HIS HARBOR GIRL

by

Rekha Ambardar

WHISKEY CREEK PRESS
www.whiskeycreekpress.com

Published by
WHISKEY CREEK PRESS

Whiskey Creek Press
PO Box 51052
Casper, WY 82605-1052
www.whiskeycreekpress.com

Copyright © 2004 by *Rekha Ambardar*

Names, characters and incidents depicted in this book are products of the author's imagination or are used fictitiously. Any resemblance to actual events, locales, organizations, or persons, living or dead, is entirely coincidental and beyond the intent of the author or the publisher.

No part of this book may be reproduced or transmitted in any form or by any means, electronic or mechanical, including photocopying, recording, or by any information storage and retrieval system, without permission in writing from the publisher.

ISBN 1-59374-192-8

Credits
Cover Artist: Sahara Kelly
Editor: Marsha Briscoe

Printed in the United States of America

Dedication

~~To all my writer friends at Outreach International Romance Writers, whose many instances of inspirational support have helped me in the writing of this book.~~

Chapter 1

A jeans-clad figure filled the doorway. Only one man in the whole universe looked like that, stood like that, and regarded Leanna in that half-rakish, half-respectful way. And only one person had broken her heart.

"Bryce!"

Leanna steadied herself by pressing her palms flat on the glass surface of the case. If she were lucky, she'd still be able to conceal how the sight of him affected her. So many times she'd wondered what she'd do if he wandered through the door. Now, here he stood at The Tug, where a new inventory of quartz pendants on black silk cord kept her busy this morning.

"What are you doing here, of all places?" She kept her voice low and steady, and even managed a smile, as if to say "no hard feelings." They were two civilized people. At least, one of them was. She should be able to handle five years' absence since the last time they had been together.

He moved closer for a second then stepped back. His glance took in her face and her cotton skirt and the near-transparent beige peasant blouse. Leanna flushed under his gaze.

"I'm here to do a study of wolves on Benedict Island. Have you forgotten what I do for a living?"

No, she hadn't. She'd just never expected him to show up here.

His Harbor Girl

He looked around the combination gift-and-supplies store with interest. Leanna concealed a grin as she took in what he saw. The pilothouse portion of it jutted out onto the lake, reminding amazed customers like him that this extraordinary structure was actually a boat. Its other end stood grounded in the sands with cement pads poured around it, the sides enveloped in walls so that it was still possible to see a clear line where they met the wall.

"Doesn't seem high enough for a boat."

"That's because we had the bottom cut off with a commercial torch." Leanna smiled at his disbelief. "The whole thing is just separate metal slabs welded together. You can cut off as many pieces of it as you want."

She watched him absorb the whiff of fresh paint that still lingered and dart a glance at the red-and-white inside that gave the whole structure a merry ambience. The boat's anchor hung on the wall adjacent to the door, like a huge dangling pendant on a dowager's necklace. Behind the counter on the wall, a miniature oil painting depicted The Tug in its previous lifetime as a boat in more somber colors—gray and dark green—serenely at anchor on a placid Lake Superior.

Bryce let out a subdued breath. "Isn't this just like you to open a store on a boat? In all the time I knew you, I never knew what you'd surprise me with next." He stared at an arrangement of a stylized fishing net and shells hanging on another wall, and a telescope, set up on a stand in front of the window, was angled toward the lake.

"The idea wasn't mine. It was Dad's. He was captain of this boat. When he retired, The Tug retired with him."

He looked around. "Small and compact." He strolled to the far side of the store, where an addition had been built, and peered into the inner recesses.

"It extends to a studio apartment my father constructed." She hung back and studied the man he'd become. The lanky, bleary-eyed student she'd loved had done a chameleon-like change into a muscular, well-built man. He was tanned from the outdoors and a red cotton bandana encircled his strong neck. His blond hair swept back from his forehead like an eagle's wings in repose, and the deep tan of his lean features set off his light gray eyes. Now he'd walked back into her life. "Why here, Bryce?"

He made a sharp half-turn at her question. "I beg your pardon?"

"Out of all the places you could have gone to, why did you come here?" She busied herself with folding tissue paper at the counter. She had to calm her nerves, and at the same time, appear unconcerned.

"You still manage to make your point. I'll give you that." He sounded amused. "To answer your question, I'm here for very professional reasons. We're doing an ongoing study of wolves on Benedict Island. There's been a decline in the population."

"And you didn't know I was here."

"No, that's not quite true." Bryce traced the lines of a wooden, white-painted seagull set on one of the shelves alongside of him.

Leanna looked at his hands, transfixed. Strong, gentle hands, she remembered.

"I thought you might be here but wasn't sure. You could have married. Did you?"

The only man she'd ever wanted to marry stood in her store. But she couldn't let herself fall for his charms a second time. Leanna toyed with one of several replies she could give as she came from behind the counter and leaned against it.

His Harbor Girl

She folded her arms and let a few seconds go by before replying. "No, I'm not. And you?"

"Me?" He stared down at the floor. For the first time since he came in, he avoided looking her in the eye. "I'm not married. Since you ran away without a word, there was no one who could fill your shoes. And it wasn't for want of trying, believe me!"

Leanna dropped her gaze and felt her stomach tighten. She could well believe that. There would have been hordes of women, given his charm; Bryce could turn it on. But she had to straighten out something first. "I had a good reason to leave." Her voice shook.

"And that's just what you did." His voice, deep and resonant, held the accusation of one who had been betrayed. "Without a word, or an address. I knew you'd be somewhere in Pelican Harbor or a town close-by."

Leanna stared at him. What would it take to make him understand the heartache of waiting endlessly for words that never came, moments stolen from a rival called work? She had made it easy for him, being there, a wife in every sense of the word, except in the legal one. "I wasn't lost, Bryce. You were. In your work."

"After you left, I wished you'd told me…"

"I did try to tell you, in so many ways. Only, you didn't want to listen, or see what was happening." She choked, making it difficult to get the words out. If only she could be anesthetized by some invisible power, instead of having to feel the pain.

"We had good times together. Have you forgotten?"

How could she forget? How they'd sit by the pond, her head on his shoulders. The warm night air as they walked down the arboretum filled with the fragrance of petunias. A shiver ran through her and she bit her lip. "Yes, there were good times. But beyond that, you hardly noticed my presence."

"Not notice your presence! That was hardly likely when every guy on campus tried to date you. Not that I blamed them, brunette beauty that you are. Keeping the guys at bay was a full time job." He took a step back and leaned against the opposite counter with the languid movements of a cougar.

A glow of satisfaction swept through her but she tried to ignore it. As if a compliment carelessly given would wipe out the emptiness of those years of bringing up Kai, now four years old.

The difficult questions Kai asked in her child's voice had hurt. Where was Daddy? Did he go to work? Would he come back with presents? Then the slow realization he wasn't ever coming back sank in. Finally, the questions stopped. In her happy, innocent way, she'd taken to talking to her stuffed toys.

Leanna picked up a duster and wiped the glass cases as the early morning light poured through the windows. She didn't want to have a customer walk in on a personal discussion between the owner and her former lover. Leanna shook her head; she didn't know how to classify him now, ex-boyfriend or husband material. A dull knock hammered in the pit of her stomach. What a laugh! Bryce as husband material.

Silence filled the empty space between them.

"You have a store to run. Since I came to buy supplies I'll pick up the things I need and get out of your way." He found what he wanted and returned to the counter.

Leanna rang up his items, put them in a white plastic bag and handed it to him.

On his way out, Bryce stopped at a shelf holding an array of ceramic creations.

Special water carafes, soap dishes, muffin plates and flower pots fired in blue glaze and inscribed with the store's name. "Very nice. Who makes these?"

"Local artisans." Why was he lingering? She clenched her teeth. It was just like Bryce to be obstinate. "If you'll excuse me."

"Of course. But I hope you and I will run into each other sometime."

Would he stay long? She steeled herself from asking, not giving him the satisfaction of seeing her curiosity.

"Are your parents well?" Interest marked Bryce's question.

"My mother died shortly after I came home."

A pause hung in the air as if waiting for a cue to vanish. Then he spoke. "I'm so very sorry."

"Thank you." Many times, over the years, she'd longed to run into his arms and be comforted. But then she had to remind herself why she'd left—he'd never been there for her when she needed him. She'd struggled to get over the double loss of her mother and Bryce, and she'd done it. She felt stronger for it now.

Leanna smiled. She wanted to part ways with him in good spirits. Whatever had happened in the past needn't make her weepy now. She was over him, and not even seeing him after all these years would destroy the peace she'd found. If her stomach tightened at the sight of him, and she felt her throat close with tension, then that was to be expected. Beyond that Bryce didn't have any power over her.

"With research you'll have your work cut out for you. And I have mine." A subtle hint like that should keep him away. She'd be all right. She'd keep to her side of the lake and he could bury himself on Benedict Island doing his study.

"I see that. You manage the store alone?"

His Harbor Girl

"My dad helps me. He's gone into town on an errand at the moment." Her father had taken Kai into town to buy her a pair of beach sandals. Something prevented Leanna from mentioning Kai, a sort of vague superstition in her own mind.

She threw a surreptitious glance at him as he stopped to examine a copper artifact. Kai. How long would it take him to figure out she was his child? Their child? She was tall for her age, but then so were both her parents. Kai's hair was a rich brown, not the thick blond shock of hair Bryce kept pushing back sometimes in an impatient gesture. Nah, Leanna told herself, Kai was her own person, not a stamped variety of anyone. A sudden breath of relief escaped from her. She'd have to keep that realization in mind if ever the thought came galloping back to haunt her—whether Bryce would guess Kai was his daughter or not.

The rumble of a car drifted in from the parking lot. Leanna turned her head, hearing female chatter as car doors slammed.

As Bryce walked toward the door, it opened with the tinkle of a bell dangling above it.

"Hello, Ida and Alice," Leanna said to two ladies.

"Good morning, ladies," Bryce said. He held the door open. "Lovely day, isn't it?"

Leanna rolled her eyes, and watched him escort them in like prize debutantes. She turned to adjust a pewter candleholder on a shelf toward the back of the gift shop. Bryce seemed determined to charm his way in and out of Pelican Harbor. He still had his easy, friendly manner with people. So, she thought with a jolt, did Kai, who took to people quickly, offering them tokens like a bunch of flowers she'd just picked. Kai's natural curiosity and interest in new things were something else that reminded her of Bryce. But then so did

His Harbor Girl

Leanna herself have these qualities; she was reading too much into everything she was seeing in Bryce.

She gave herself a mental shake. She couldn't deny the wariness she felt, coupled with the undeniable attraction. But the store and Kai were the most important things to her, and she'd see to it that it stayed that way. Bryce didn't fit in the picture, not the way things stood between them.

Still she could stand there watching him forever. But it was a workday, despite Bryce having dropped in from nowhere. She had to get a hold of herself and keep Bryce and Kai apart in her mind—for now.

Bryce turned, waved, then sauntered out of the store.

"Who was that young man?" Ida asked.

"He's a scientist who's come to do research on Benedict Island. He's well known for his study on wolves. He's even been on the evening news."

Leanna turned to the older of the two ladies. "Alice, thanks for helping with Kai so much. You really must let me pay you."

"Oh, I couldn't take money. You, Chester and Kai are like family to me."

"That's very sweet of you."

"It's quite all right to need one another, dear." Alice ran her fingers through her short, gray curls. She had a round, cherubic face and blinked constantly from behind thick glasses.

Leanna remembered with fondness Alice and Gerald's "adoption" of her, her dad and Kai when Leanna's mother died. And when Gerald had died, she and her father had rallied round Alice. To their surprise, she had made a valiant recovery from grief.

"What's the use of being glum?" Alice would say. "You wouldn't have an ant's chance if you didn't pick yourself up and move on."

That seemed like sound advice to Leanna, who was still trying to get over her own loss.

Ida busied herself going through the store. "I'm looking for a birthday present for my niece. You've got some really pretty things here."

"Thank you. Look around all you want and let me know when you find something." The nervous excitement that Bryce had caused was gone now. She'd willed it away.

Lately, the store had been taking in a good amount of money with the tourist season gradually approaching. Motor and sailboats were anchored at the pier. Recreational vehicles rolled in with visitors from Ontario and Lower Michigan to scout around for a suitable camping ground or just to enjoy the lakeside beauty of Pelican Harbor. Fat gulls strutted on the road, bleached white from the salt sprayed on it during winter, and waited expectantly for tourists and other pedestrians to throw breadcrumbs.

Alice approached the counter, smiling with the elation of a party announcer. "Nolan Packard asked if I would pass on a message to you. He tried calling you."

"Oh?" Leanna had been introduced to him at the Chamber of Commerce office when she dropped off a few hand-printed brochures about The Tug. What could he have to say to her? Probably he was just looking for an excuse to ask her out. She hadn't missed the look of admiration he had shot at her.

Ida emerged from a corner, where she had been crouched looking at lacey scrimshaw work letter openers. "Isn't he that developer?"

"Yes."

After a few minutes of browsing, the ladies left.

A steady stream of customers kept Leanna busy at the cash register, which was good for business. She didn't like the days when business dragged at a snail's pace. On such days, she washed the windows and looked over the inventory to see if anything needed reordering.

Toward noon, Leanna heard the sound of the back door opening and the heavy tread of hiking boots accompanied by the quicker sound of a child's footsteps.

"Hello!" A deep voice boomed with the authority of a foghorn making its presence known in pea soup fog.

"Dad? In here."

A gruff, white-bearded man and a little girl clutching a parcel entered the store.

"Did you have fun, baby?" Leanna smoothed away wisps of hair from Kai's face with a tender touch and knelt down to unzip her mauve jacket.

Kai nodded in reply, her curls bobbing. "Look what Gramps bought for me." She sat on the floor and opened a small box to reveal a pair of sandals with a net-like plastic weave on top.

"They're lovely. Now you can wade in the shallow water when you go looking for starfish and colored agate."

"Of course, she had to try all of them and then decide. She's as hard to please as her mother at that age. You did the same thing when you were little. Your mother and I would have a time of it taking you shopping."

The box containing her sandals tucked under one arm and a stuffed Eeyore under the other, Kai retreated to a corner of the store. Leanna had spread a blanket there, out of sight of the customers. There were a small plastic chair and an assortment of toys for her daughter. She'd keep herself busy for an hour. When she became restless, Leanna would have to dream up some other occupation for her.

"How's business been, Lea?"

"Steady. And the researchers have arrived."

"The ones coming to Benedict Island? That's going to be interesting. Will they need ferry service to the island? I'll have to tell Marcum's Marina to expect more passengers."

"Don't know if they'll be needing the ferry service or not. I met only one of them." Leanna tried to slip the information in casually. Her father hadn't known about Bryce. She had not wanted to discuss their affair with him. It would have been different if her mother were alive because Leanna might have confided in her. As dearly as she loved her father, she knew there was nothing he could do about it. And she hadn't wanted to tell him who Kai's father was. Fortunately, he had just accepted the situation with his offer of moral support, turning over the cottage to her and Kai. He constructed a small annex to the store, which served as an apartment for him.

"Just so you and Kai will have a place to yourselves," he'd said. "Now that Mother is gone, all I need is a little bit of space."

"But you don't have to do that, Dad."

"You girls need a place of your own. You don't want an old geezer in the way."

It had only been a year since The Tug was up and running. Until then, Leanna had her hands full taking care of Kai. Then, Kai emerged from the baby stage and left Leanna free to think of opening a store.

"You going to take tourists to the island?" Chester walked outside with her.

A small garden bench stood facing the lake. Here Kai had spread out her sandals, Eeyore and some small, pearly shells she'd found under a nearby sand heap.

"Yes, I think so. Especially if it doesn't interfere with being at the store." Leanna loved the open trails, the trill of the birds, the enormous maples forming a canopy above. Since she had taken people to the island last summer, the Park

Service Office at Pelican Harbor made her a standing offer to do it every year, if she had time. "Wish I could take Cody there too, but that's not allowed. Too bad he's cooped up at home."

Cody was all she had from the time she'd known Bryce, before she'd known she was pregnant. Cody was part of Bryce too. She and Bryce had gone together to look at puppies and came away with a frisky three-month old bundle, part husky, part Labrador retriever. The landlady had allowed Leanna to keep Cody. How could she refuse, when Cody, a large ball of fur, had snuggled up to her? That was when she noticed that Cody had silver-gray eyes—and so had Bryce.

Until she saw Bryce again, she'd forgotten how light his eyes were. Light and powerful wolf's eyes that gave him a strange kinship with the animals he researched with meticulous care.

* * * *

The meeting with Leanna had unsettled Bryce's well-ordered life, even though he had assured himself he'd be able to handle it if he found her. He hadn't been quite honest when he told Leanna that he didn't know she'd be running a gift shop. Of course, he'd known she lived in Pelican Harbor, and a few inquiries at the Chamber of Commerce had told him about The Tug and who owned it.

He made his way now to the Pelican Harbor Park Service office, a brisk walk of about a mile, where the rest of his research associates, two graduate students and another scientist, Fred Schultz, were waiting. Anchored motorboats rocked gently against the whitewashed docks of Marcum's Marina in a parallel array of white and gray. The lakefront had the look of an artist's creation on an inspired day.

A collection of duffel bags and assorted sleeping bags lay piled in a corner of the office, which had only enough space for a large desk and the national flag standing on a brass pole capped by a carved bald eagle. Maps of Benedict Island in relation to Michigan and Wisconsin covered the entire wall on one side.

Fred caught Bryce's elbow. "We could have come a few days later. Marcum, the man who runs the *Benedict Island Queen* service, has taken a freighter carrying cargo out to the main harbor."

Bryce could barely suppress his annoyance. "So now, we sit here and wait, when we have to set up for wolf tracking. We should be moving into the cabins we've leased. We can't have all this state-of-the-art equipment lying idle."

The Park Service office clerk overheard them. "There is somebody else who can take you. Chester Reed, the man who owns The Tug, is a seasoned sailor. He could be persuaded to run you gentlemen up to the island."

"Reed?" Fred looked doubtful while the two students, Clyde and Tim, hung about listlessly chewing gum.

"It's all right," Bryce said. "I know him…that is, I know his daughter."

Fred stared at him, surprised. "I thought you didn't know anyone here."

"Well, it's a long story." Bryce tried not to give himself away. The thought of the way Leanna's dark hair fell back from her face when she looked up at him brought a heated flush to his face. He snatched up a duffel bag and forced himself to concentrate on what needed to be done. He couldn't afford to think of Leanna now.

* * * *

The phone trilled in The Tug office. Leanna hurried to pick it up while glancing at a couple of customers who were looking at postcards and picture books about ships that had plied Lake Superior in the nineteenth century.

His Harbor Girl

"Hello?" Leanna balanced the receiver on her shoulder and cleared the counter of envelopes and wrapping paper.

A deep voice came over the line. "Leanna, we have a favor to ask."

"Bryce!" What did he want now?

"Can Chester ferry us across to Benedict Island? Marcum's gone on another job. The Park Service mentioned your father could take us."

It was flattering that the Park Service office had recommended her father. But her father suffered from occasional arthritis, enough to keep away from many of his previous occupations. "Maybe he could handle a one-time passage across the lake. I have to ask him and let you know."

Leanna hung up, her heart still pounding. Was this going to be the pattern for the duration of Bryce's stay? Her plan of keeping her life private was already flying out the window.

She went to the back of the store. "Dad, could you come in here, please?"

The back door opened and Chester walked in, wiping gnarled hands on a piece of rag. He had mentioned that he was finishing up the varnishing job on the rocking chair he liked so much. His nails were cracked and blackened from drywalling, painting and sawing. It had taken a lot of work to make the addition to the store.

"The new group that's come to work on the island needs to be ferried across. Marcum's away and there's nobody else."

"Well...I wanted to pull up a loose board from the siding."

Part of her wanted to see Bryce again and read his mind, look into those eyes half-amused, half-questioning. If only she hadn't been so headstrong and had run away without so much as a phone call. She'd been young, easily hurt, and hurtful.

She'd wanted to hurt Bryce as much as she thought she had been hurt.

That was so long ago. A rogue thought now shot through her mind. She was actually happy to see him, but darned if she'd let him know that.

"Actually, I know one of them." Leanna was reluctant to mention Bryce.

"That so? Who?" Chester looked surprised. Apart from their usual group of friends, Leanna never talked of anybody else before.

"Bryce Robertson. I knew him in college."

Chester's eyes lost their piercing sharpness and a look of compassion crossed his face. He wasn't one to question her and she wondered what he read into her remark.

"Did you now! Was he your special young man in college?"

"Sort of. But we lost touch. You know how it is in college. You meet, get to know one another, and then you take different paths." Leanna made sure there was just the right touch of nonchalance in her tone, but she knew she couldn't fool her father. There was the same amount of devil-may-care in her tone when she'd returned from college suddenly and told her father she was pregnant. She had sensed that Chester saw the pain, but kept from intruding.

"I've never been to college, little girl, but I see how new falutin' ideas can send people in different ways."

Leanna had been amazed to find wisdom in the man who disappeared from her life for months on end. If only he had been there once in a while to guide her with his wisdom when she was growing up.

"Are you going to take them across?"

He nodded. "They are guests here, and for a good reason. I'll take them across. Want to come?"

"No, Alice is bringing Kai home from preschool and I should be here. Better call the Park Service office and let the clerk know you'll be there."

She didn't quite know why she was pushing Chester to help Bryce and his associates. Perhaps she didn't want to appear inhospitable and deny his request. Besides, what could possibly result from taking them across except Bryce owing them one?

Leanna couldn't help noticing that her father had the same caring look he used to have during his short shore leaves when he used to take her on hikes through the woods as a child. Those moments made her remember her father with fondness in the times he left her mother and her for endless months.

Leanna would just as soon not see Bryce again for a while, if she could help it.

* * * *

Bryce and his colleagues hauled their luggage, supplies and equipment onto the pier. He'd received word from the Park Service office clerk that Chester Reed had agreed to ferry them to Benedict Island.

Bryce returned to the office to see they weren't leaving anything behind.

"Tourist traffic hasn't started yet. Some folks come early but Marcum takes them across every few days. But you gentlemen shouldn't have to wait."

"We really appreciate your help. And you're right, we've got to get started on the work."

"Anything you need, call us here." The clerk pointed to the phone on a crowded desk. The next moment he looked doubtful. "Are you even on a phone line?"

Bryce patted the pocket of his blue fleece jacket. "I have a cell phone. And thanks, if we need anything, we'll call."

He walked out of the office and saw a burly older man sporting a white beard approach him.

"Good afternoon, I'm Chester Reed. You folks need to be taken to the island?"

Bryce nodded and extended his hand. "Bryce Robertson."

Chester grinned and shook his hand. "Got a lot of luggage, I see." He helped them load the small blue and white steamboat that stood anchored alongside the dock.

"No vehicles allowed on the island."

"We don't need any."

Chester cast off and steered the ferry slowly away from the shore.

"Always glad to meet a friend of Lea's."

"Pardon?" Bryce wasn't sure what to make of Chester's comment.

"Lea says she knew you in college."

"Ah…yes. And I'm glad to meet you. Are you her father?"

Chester nodded but kept his eyes on the course as the shoreline shrank in the distance. "Yessir, she's always busy with the store. It's good for her. That and her daughter."

Bryce jerked his head toward Chester, surprised to hear that Leanna had a daughter. She hadn't mentioned that, and it could have been why she had left without a word. He was sure if this were his child, Leanna would have told him. A thought crept into his mind. Maybe, she didn't tell him because the father was someone from their college days. No, couldn't be, because he knew all of them. Well, then she'd met somebody here in Pelican Harbor. A dull feeling overcame him. He knew why and didn't want to give it a name. He'd been smacked by the monster called jealousy before, but never like this.

His Harbor Girl

    Bryce pushed away his thoughts for now and glanced at Chester, whose grasp tightened on the thick steering wheel. He composed himself and said, "Her daughter?"

    "Yuh, Leanna's crazy about that kid." Chester gave the boat's steering wheel a gradual turn.

Chapter 2

Leanna parked her car outside the Beef 'n' Brew to pick up a soup and sandwich for Kai. As she was about to enter, Dick Langtry, the Park Service Supervisor, walked out.

"Hi, Leanna!"

"Hello, Dick. Late lunch again?"

He nodded. "Just packed off that new bunch of scientists who came in. They had an impressive set of equipment. Did you meet them? By the way, please thank Chester for taking them over."

"I met one of them. And I'll tell my father." Leanna was amused at the way his mind sprang from one thought to another, which was just the way he functioned.

She'd learned to keep up with that from working with him during past summers.

"We've had requests for tourist tickets to Benedict Island. You still available to take them over?"

"I can't, because of the store. But if I had enough notice, I'd be glad to."

The store was her life; beyond that, she didn't have any. Since when did she care about a personal life? Bryce. He'd been here only a short while and already she was thinking about things better left alone. Leanna's hand curled over the car keys in her pocket.

"Of course." He pulled out a large handkerchief, wiped his glasses and put them back on. "You know, I'm glad those guys are here, especially this Bryce Robertson. He's big in scientific circles. It'll put Pelican Harbor on the map."

Leanna fidgeted with the ring on her pinky finger but answered with outward calm. "As far as I'm concerned, Pelican Harbor is already on the map. It's where I grew up."

"Don't I remember that? You were just a toddler when I came to work here, and now my family and I don't want to be anywhere else."

"That's the spirit." Leanna was possessive about Pelican Harbor. It was her home, her sanctuary after the split with Bryce.

He peered at her through his glasses. "Well, I must be off. And I don't want to keep you from getting lunch."

"Keep me posted about the tour."

Fifteen minutes later, she drove back to the store, feeling a swell of pride for her hometown. She'd come back and was pleased with her decision to stay, even though she could have earned more money as a tech assistant examining cell structure in some company lab. In her small way, she contributed to the community effort of beautifying Pelican Harbor by opening The Tug with its nautical decor.

She turned into the small parking space behind the store and noticed that Chester's truck wasn't in its usual spot.

He wasn't yet back from ferrying Bryce and the others to the island. Leanna let herself in through the back entrance and found Alice at the cash register wrapping up a gilt-trimmed white ceramic mug for a customer. Kai was playing with her toys in the hideaway play area and ran to Leanna when she saw her.

"Soup and sandwich for you." She set the package on the small chair for her daughter.

"How's it been?" she asked Alice.

"Just a few browsers now and then. I sold a couple of ashtrays and just now a coffee mug. Where's Chester?" Alice watched Leanna pour herself some coffee.

"Gone to the island with the research group."

"You mean that young man who was in here this morning?"

Leanna nodded. "Bryce Robertson." Strange how good it felt to say his name. "There are three others with him. Marcum's been called away and there was nobody else to take them to Benedict Island."

Alice's eyes twinkled. "Such a nice young man. So rare to find such well-mannered young men nowadays. I don't mean to tell you what to do, dear, but since your mother died you haven't given yourself a chance to meet somebody nice. First, you were bringing up Kai. Now the store takes up all your time."

"I'm grateful for your concern, but I'm fine—really."

Her choice of a vocation and way of life must have seemed remarkably dull to Alice and, maybe, even to her father, although he'd never mentioned it.

"Now, take that young Bryce Robertson. He's going to make some girl a fine husband."

Leanna wheeled around. "Bryce married?" There was a fine contradiction! Her lower lip trembled. Memories that she'd ignored now assaulted her.

Alice was like a mother to her and Leanna wanted her to know about Bryce. How would she take it? There was only one way to find out.

"There's something I have to tell you." Leanna forced herself to count to twenty. Then, standing on tiptoe, she looked over the far end of the counter at Kai. She needn't have worried. Kai, her childish lips set in a thin line, was scolding Eeyore for throwing a tantrum. "I used to know Bryce."

"You did?" Alice's eyes widened. "And?"

"He was not ready for a commitment at the time."

"That's why you came home?"

Leanna nodded. "Mom was ill, too, as I found out later."

Alice lowered her voice. "Kai is Bryce's child, isn't she?"

"How did you know?"

"Wasn't hard to figure out. Does Chester know?"

Leanna shook her head. "It was all too complicated back then. Besides, with Mom being ill, he had plenty to think about and I didn't want to worry him with my problems. Anyway, I don't regret what happened because I have Kai now. When I met Bryce, I thought it was the most wonderful thing. He knew what he wanted and went after it. I first saw him sitting on the floor at a party, holding a discussion on parvo viral infection in wolves."

"Is that the type of infection that dogs get if they stay too long in the woods?"

Leanna nodded in admiration. For all her fluttery ways, Alice was well informed. Many were the times that Leanna had hoped that her father would cultivate a friendship with her; Alice would smooth over his rough edges. But he had yet to reciprocate Alice's friendly and thoughtful overtures.

"I remember his hair was a mess, and he wore jeans and a white shirt with a button missing. Yet his eyes shone with an excitement which he would have had even if he were looking at lightning bugs in a jar."

Alice appeared disappointed. "That's how you met? A handsome devil like that?"

Leanna shrugged. "At the time I thought I'd have a better chance of getting to know him if I were a wolf."

Alice laughed. "I'll say!"

"Then one day he called out of the blue and asked if I wanted to go to a movie. Some new movie, I forget which."

"Did it get better?"

"Oh, yes." Leanna chuckled. Alice was positively drooling. "He took me everywhere, not just out for a date, but to his lab to look at specimens under microscope. His work occupied him most of the time, and I was flattered that he wanted to share all that with me."

"And then?" Alice angled her head to listen more intently.

"That went on for a while. Then, all of a sudden, it was as if I was no more important than lab equipment. I would have followed him anywhere, but he wasn't ready to call it permanent."

Alice shook her head. "I'm so sorry."

"And I wasn't going to force him. That's when I came home and found out Mom was ill."

"You weren't talking much then, I noticed. You looked pale. I wondered if something was wrong."

Leanna remembered her listlessness. About that time she knew she was pregnant. All those Saturday evenings spent at Bryce's apartment filled with books, pictures of specimens viewed under the electron-scanning microscope. She'd gotten him to listen to tapes of Dave Bruebeck's piano and the cool sax of Acker Bilk. He'd be tender and passionate one moment. The next minute, he was back to the paper he had to prepare for a conference, bursting the bubble of the sense of closeness between them.

"Kai has your coloring but her father's features. Does he know?"

Leanna's palms felt sweatier. Alice had asked the dreaded question. "No, he doesn't." If Alice could see Kai's resemblance to Bryce, wouldn't he do the same? And if he did he would probably ask for visitation rights to his child. That would be the end of the ordered life Leanna had carved for herself and Kai almost out of nothing.

"When are you going to tell him?"

"When the time is right." She wasn't ready to think about it just yet. Later, perhaps. But she had no idea when that would be. Or if it made it any easier now that he had re-entered her life.

The low roar of a pickup truck told Leanna that her father would be trudging in with his arms full of bags of tools or groceries.

Leanna jumped up, opened the front door, and looked out. The sand-washed road that lay like a gray ribbon off to the side of the store was deserted. No more customers, she decided. She locked the door from the inside, hung the "Closed" sign, and went into the back, where she could hear Chester moving about in his apartment.

Presently, he came out. "See what Gramps got for you, Kai." He held out a small bag of chocolate chip cookies.

"Dad, you shouldn't have."

"Don't worry about it because I ate some of them. You young people fret too much about diet. Don't you agree, Alice?"

"I don't know the meaning of the word." Alice's face lit up.

Leanna grinned at Alice's attempts at getting Chester to chat with her. Her father was usually too busy with his carpentry projects to slow down and notice what went on around him.

Alice walked toward the back door. "Well, I'll see you later."

Leanna smiled and waved. Alice lived close by, two houses down in a ranch-style home shaded by maples. It was a house that Leanna had watched Gerald construct with little help from anyone else.

She and Kai followed Chester into his apartment, which resembled the inside of a boat. A steering wheel hung from the ceiling like a fan. Shells of every shape and color were arranged on a low wooden shelf that he'd built. A sign on the wall that said "Welcome Aboard" completed the eccentric decor.

"I hauled them over to the island safe and sound. The luggage they had!"

"They're here for work, Dad. From what I hear, they'll be here a while."

"That young Robertson seemed interested in our store. Nobody expects to see a boat turned into a store."

Her ears perked up. Was it really the store he was interested in? "What did he say?"

"Just asked how long you had it. Then he turned odd when I said you had gone off to get something for Kai."

"You mentioned Kai?"

Her father nodded. "He asked who Kai was, so I told him."

Leanna turned and stashed the groceries in the small refrigerator occupying part of a space that served as the living and dining area.

Chester caught her sharp movement. "What's the matter?"

"Oh, nothing. Maybe he was just surprised that I have Kai. We lost touch after college."

"Pleasant young man. Seems well educated. None of the arrogance that goes with it."

No arrogance. Just an absent-minded carelessness of people around him. And now wasn't the time to pick up the pieces of their annihilated relationship, if that was what Bryce was thinking.

"Yes, he's that. The food is all put away. I'm off now. By the way, Dad, you might take time to chat with Alice now and then. She likes you."

"I know. She's a good woman. But I'm too busy with carpentry. Furniture World is buying small items from me on consignment."

"Then go for it, since your carpentry work keeps you busy and happy."

Leanna led Kai out of the apartment. Left to herself, Kai could spend hours playing with the nautical ornaments that littered her father's comical apartment. It reminded Leanna of the Popeye movie she'd seen, and it had the fuzzy warmth the setting in the movie had exhibited.

"Back tomorrow," Leanna called out over her shoulder.

"See my favorite girls later."

As she walked up the hill with Kai skipping along beside her, Leanna felt a swell of reassurance when she thought of the change in her father since her mother's death. She savored the moment. How unfortunate that her mother had never experienced it because of his long maritime journeys.

As she and Kai mounted the hill she heard seagulls cackle in unison. They flew and swooped down fearlessly and skipped in the lake behind her. She smiled at the cacophony around her and entered the walkway of her cottage. It was an old, bungalow-style cottage with a gabled roof and a porch in front. Her father had bought it for a song and painted it a pale mauve, at her mother's request. Delicate white curtains completed the ensemble.

Leanna spied Cody at the long living room window, resting his paws on the sill, staring at them in anticipation. Kai waved to him and he bounced with wild abandon at the window, tail wagging at raving speed.

Leanna unlocked the door and watched him come tearing up to them, licking their faces when mother and daughter knelt down to pet him. "Have you been cooped up all day? Does Cody want to go for a walk?"

"Yeah, let's." Kai bounced like a ball at Leanna's side.

"Fetch your leash, Cody."

Cody trotted obediently into a smaller area by the living room and returned with a leather leash between his teeth and sat in front of Leanna with his front paws up, begging.

"Good boy!"

Kai and Cody leaped out of the front door and Leanna pulled it shut.

The road rounded the contours of the hill as it dipped in a silent curtsey toward the lake. The trio made their way toward the water, still as a sheet of blue glass. A sailboat or two bobbed on the water.

"Will we go to the island?" Kai asked.

Her daughter's question was a sudden wake-up call to Leanna. "The island? I don't know."

"Will you take people there?"

"I suppose so." Her throat constricted. She hadn't thought about how she'd do that and keep out of sight of Bryce at the same time. She might run into him when she took tourists there. The thought filled her with caution, especially under her new resolve of going full steam ahead with her own life.

* * * *

The week after their arrival at the island found Bryce and his colleagues settled comfortably in their cabins. The two students shacked up in one, Bryce and Fred settled in the other. It had two small bedrooms with a common bathroom, a comfortable living area heated by a fireplace, a propane stove for cooking, and a shelf on the wall for food.

A drafting table served as Bryce's desk. On it were laptop computer, assorted pens, pencils and rulers. Two or three thick reference books bulged with typewritten notes stuck in between the pages.

Fred sat on a stool whittling away on a long piece of wood he had found when they went out exploring. Bryce glanced at him. "You sure that's going to make a fine walking stick?'

"Of course, I'm sure. This is a great way to go up and down hills and trails. Less trauma on the knees. 'Cos, face it, man, you and I aren't getting any younger."

Bryce grinned. "Isn't that the truth?" Fred could pass as a lumberjack with his shoulder-length hair pulled back in a ponytail. He wore a faded red plaid shirt half tucked into his jeans. But all that was misleading. He had a razor-sharp mind and was an asset in their research.

"It was nice of Reed to bring us here, but, you know, Bryce…"

"I know. We can't rely on public transportation to take us back and forth from the mainland. It's a good forty miles and that will take up a lot of time. I've asked for a light plane and a pilot who'll stay for brief periods of time. They've promised us that should we need it." Bryce took a cell phone out of his pocket and placed it on the table.

"That's a relief. We can cover more distance from a plane and it's easier to spot wolves."

Bryce helped himself to another cup of coffee from the coffee pot. They'd had a full day scouting the area. All four of them had eaten venison stew Fred had prepared from the frozen meat he'd brought along.

"So, how long have you known her?"

"Who?" Bryce feigned wide-eyed ignorance.

"Reed's daughter."

Bryce let a few moments slip by. "We were in college together for a while."

Fred jerked his head up. "Really? And what was she doing there?"

"Studying, like everyone else. But then she gave up and left in a hurry."

Fred gave him a mock-serious look. "If you're looking for advice, old Uncle Fred has a remedy for what ails you."

"And what's that?"

"Lose yourself in work. But I don't have to tell you that."

Bryce chuckled. "No, you don't. Coffee?"

"Later. By the way, did you give Reed our cell phone number?"

"Yes. Just in case somebody wants to get a hold of us and doesn't know our whereabouts. Like family members."

"Now, you're making it sound as if we're in a line of work fraught with danger."

Bryce said in a level voice. "Just a precaution." He got up and went to the sink where the plates had been washed and stacked. He put them in the shelf overhead.

He had been busy all day each day, but he couldn't squelch the questions at the back of his mind—how long Leanna had been a single mother and who Kai's father was. When Chester had mentioned Kai, Bryce had to steady himself to absorb that piece of information. Even though Leanna had denied that she was married, now thinking of it, there had been a tentativeness to her reply when he asked. She'd also appeared even more unapproachable than he'd imagined.

Bryce returned to the worktable and started rifling through his notes. He had hoped to find her here after all those years of her puzzling disappearance and silence. When his wolf study had offered him an opportunity, his desire to find her redoubled. He'd even questioned himself as to how he'd let her slip away from his life in the first place. In the back of his mind, though, he wasn't sure he would find her, but it was worth a serious attempt. As for picking up the threads again with Leanna, that didn't look promising at all.

He opened up his laptop and retrieved a file. He pulled out a sheet of paper from one of the thick books on the table and glanced at the data, then keyed some of them into his computer. Bryce scrolled down to view the pictures he had scanned in. Pictures of wolf pups, a pack of wolves running across snowy terrain. The first wolf pack from Benedict Island to catch the world's attention nearly forty years ago.

"The Big Pack," Bryce muttered.

"What's that?" Fred turned a puzzled glance at his colleague.

"I'm looking at an original of the snapshot of a wolf pack that appeared in the *National Geographic* years ago."

"Not many researchers have come here in recent years. But now, since you've rattled their cages about it, they are looking this way."

Bryce continued his pensive study of the pictures until his scrolling brought onto the screen the picture of a svelte brunette laughing at the photographer. Bryce's hand fell from the keyboard. A photo of Leanna appeared on the screen. He stared at the picture and shook his head, half-ashamed. What had he let go from his life? And what a fool he had been. They'd always been together at college, ever since he'd garnered up enough guts to call her and ask her to a movie. When he hadn't the time to take her out, she'd gone along with him to the law library, an ornate building that almost looked like a medieval cathedral. He used to go there to look up DNR regulations and Leanna would bring along her own work.

The summer they'd met was the best. After staring at lab specimens all day they'd go to the outdoor café for pizza and ale.

In the picture, she leaned back against blooms of lilacs, and laughed at Bryce photographing her. She made fun of his picture taking. "You've taken so many wolf pictures that you don't know how to photograph humans!"

Bryce sat there lost in a long tunnel of memories, back to when he first knew her. A warm summer evening, darkening with the scent of lilacs and the fragrance of the English lavender perfume that she used. The smoothness of her skin, the dark silk of her hair, falling in chestnut ripples, the sweet warmth of her kisses. He'd never let on even to himself that her sudden flight had hurt him. Ever the cool intellectual, he'd forged ahead with work and life, and dated around. Except that the slinkier the women who came on to him, the more he edged away, until he retreated into his work completely.

He had carried her picture in the wallet, and then, when she left, he'd put it in the desk drawer at the office, until he scanned in photos of wolves and pups. Then he'd scanned in Leanna's photo also on a whim. Later, he realized it was not really on a whim. In the back of his mind he worried that with all the traveling he'd lose the picture, so he'd stored it in the desk drawer. And now, here she was again in front of him, reminding him of those early days, which he could almost reach out and touch. He stared at her photo, which was all he had of her. Obviously, she had picked up the reins of her life, which didn't include him.

He closed the file and got up. Weariness dragged him down, a sort of mental weariness, not the happy, tired feeling that resulted from a full day of work. For all his panache when he'd talked to Leanna that day at The Tug, he could tell she had changed from the compliant girl he'd known. But even in

His Harbor Girl

the wildest of dreams he hadn't pictured her with a child. A muscle twitched in his cheek as he pushed away papers that balanced on the edge of the desk.

"You've been quiet. What you doin' there?" Fred got up with his newly whittled walking stick.

"Compiling earlier data." Bryce forced a grin. Damned if he was going to let Fred see a picture of Leanna among his photos.

"There. Now I'm ready for tracking wolves."

"You're using that in the research plane when we get one?" Bryce couldn't help a sly dig.

"Of course not. On the ground."

"Let's get a good night's rest. Work starts tomorrow." Bryce headed toward his room, a Spartan affair comprising a low, wooden bed with a thick mattress and a dresser for clothes. But he'd piled it high with books and papers. He spent more time finding space for his books while on his field trips than he cared to remember.

He pulled off his shirt and jeans and threw himself on the bed and winced when he realized that this wasn't the box spring queen-sized number he had at home. Propping up the two meager pillows, he leaned back, threw his arm above the head, and stared at the markings on the wall's wood paneling. The bedside lamp gave the room a warm, cocoon-like atmosphere, something that would be conducive to sleep, if he could stop thinking about Leanna.

Getting to know her again was going to be an uphill battle. Good luck, he thought. He switched off the lamp and turned on his side. He would need it.

Chapter 3

Leanna slung her lightweight backpack over her shoulder and accompanied the campers onto a ramp leading to the *Benedict Island Queen*, piloted by Marcum. The Park Service had asked if she would go along with the campers to ensure that they were introduced to the pristine facilities of the island with the least amount of shock.

"Besides," Dick Langtry had said, "that way, we'll be showing them that we have an eye on them too. And then, maybe, they'll leave the island the way they found it—clean."

She had thrown in a pair of binoculars, a small bottle of water and a book, along with a map of the island. She'd be returning to the mainland in the evening on the *Queen*.

As they drifted away from the mainland, Leanna looked up at the powder blue sky. She stood on the bridge with Marcum as he steered the eighty-foot boat through a canal, after which it widened into a vast expanse of water.

"You can tell those folks they can rest easy for a while. It'll be an hour and a half before we reach the island. You have your work cut out for you with tourists starting to come in."

He was right. Tourist season had started in earnest and visitors swarmed Pelican Harbor and ambled down Main Street. They wanted to go to the island, some from curiosity and some from being hardcore campers.

Leanna looked at the small group of young men and women carrying heavy backpacks that probably contained tents and supplies. They would, no doubt, be hiking and camping in designated areas on the island.

Before boarding the *Queen*, she had assembled them in the Park Service office for a reminder. "I'd like to go over the rules on the island. No fires allowed, all trash must be carried out, not burned or buried, and no dumping wastewater into any streams or the lake."

As they boarded, Leanna told them, "An hour and a half until we reach the island. So just relax and enjoy the boat ride."

Her gaze wandered idly over the passing scenery. Then, she stiffened, wondering if she'd run into Bryce.

The boat finally approached the sandy dockside landing of Chippewa Bay. All around them the land had blossomed into lush greenery. A small wooden shed, painted white, served as a point of entry and departure for campers and other visitors to Benedict Island. Here the boat docked and its passengers disembarked.

"Okay, ladies and gentlemen, let's assemble here for a few minutes before we go in different directions." Leanna looked at a group of faces turned expectantly toward her. She knew they were eager to get going and didn't want a lecture from the tour attendant, but she still had to do her bit.

"For those of you who don't want to hike it all the way, there are at least two ferries that circumnavigate the island, the *Osprey* and the *Voyager*, which start at the other end of Lake Superior at Grand Huron. After arriving at Boulder Ridge both vessels sail around the island in a clockwise direction. You can use either of them to go from one point to the other."

After she finished briefing them, the group trudged off into the woods in different directions, leaving her heady with the essence of freedom. She wished Kai could have come along. But she had left her with Alice, who wanted to work on her garden today and had invited Kai to help.

Leanna came to a clearing in the woods where a row of shops stood with colorful window displays. Through the window she saw a toy moose, which would make a nice present for Kai. She went inside, bought it and followed the trails again.

A mellow scent of wild flowers and birch bark filled the air, made sweeter by the sun's warmth. The woods were getting denser. She heard footsteps on the thick layer of leaves. She turned around but nobody was there. The yelp of a puppy came from a distance. *Stop it; you're imagining things,* she told herself. But the footsteps continued, heavy and persistent. Then, a deep voice made her turn back and look straight into Bryce's bemused eyes.

"Well, now, I've seen everything. Instead of wolf tracks, I run right into a woodland nymph."

Leanna choked back her annoyance at being taken unawares and hearing Bryce cough up a silly remark like that. She felt gauche, lacking in control. She tugged at her khaki shirt to make sure it hadn't crumpled up at the waist.

"What are *you* doing here?" She probably sounded like a den mother scolding a cub scout who had sneaked off without telling her.

Bryce laughed and raked his gaze over her. His jacket pocket held an assortment of pens and pencils and short rulers, and he carried a duffel bag that looked half empty.

Leanna glanced behind him and around the tree-shaded thicket; certain she'd see a puppy.

"What are you looking for?" Bryce looked behind him and then around the area.

His Harbor Girl

"I thought I heard a puppy." She expected him to laugh outright at the wildness of her imagination.

"Matter of fact, behind that clump of trees there's a den with wolf pups. That's probably the yelping you heard. Wolves mate sometime in February and the female delivers the pups in April. By late summer they're practically adolescents."

He shouldered the duffel bag he had let drop to the ground. "I was looking in on the new family when I saw you."

"Were you following me?"

"Of course. A beautiful woman alone in the wilderness. I was just making sure you'd be okay." There was not the slightest hint of embarrassment in his outrageous claim.

Leanna laughed in spite of herself.

"I was hoping it would be you."

"Really? Why?"

"To show you what I do here." He threw open his arms. "This is my work space in a manner of speaking. I want you to see it, like I used to want you to see my lab back in civilization. But here we're looking at animals in their natural habitat. Here is where life is really lived."

Leanna flushed at his mention of their time together all those years ago. He hadn't forgotten. Neither had she forgotten the passion and the fervor with which he had introduced her to his life of scientific study. She had been flattered that he had thought of her as an intellectual equal. But that hadn't been enough.

"Life also includes houses, mortgage payments and grocery bills."

"You have a way of turning the tables on me." A muscle twitched in his jaw. "Nothing compares with life in the raw as here in the woods. Let me show you."

Bryce held out a hand as naturally as if he were beckoning to a child. "Come on. You're going to have a rare treat. You'll like wolf pups."

His hand, firm, protective, clasping hers made her senses spin. Breathless though she was, Leanna allowed herself to be carried away by the charade that she encountered wolf pups every day.

He led her by the hand as they tiptoed their way over thick roots and mats of damp leaves, trying not to make a sound.

"We don't usually go looking for pups in the spring. Disturbing the dens at that time might harm the pups, being so young. But in the summer, we try to approach the dens to count the pups by listening to their howling."

Leanna walked alongside Bryce, her hand still in his, although he seemed unaware of it in his quest for the den. His tread slowed and softened his footfalls. He put a finger to his lips, stopped short, and pointed to a spot darkened by tree shade, so that the whole area looked like a cave. From where they stood they saw a wolf and her pups, small, gray and white little things tumbling around the mother.

Leanna backed away as though stung by a scorpion. Cute as they were, they symbolized what tore Bryce and her apart.

"This is as far as we go." Bryce seemed to note her sudden reserve.

He took out a small notebook and scribbled something in it. "We try to identify the den sites by giving them names. When the newborn pups appear, wolf packs shift from being nomads to a more settled way of life. Come on, let's get out of here."

"Interesting you should say that," Leanna said once they were out of the den's vicinity.

"Why?"

"Aren't humans the same way too?"

"Except that their lives become more complicated when their minds intrude."

Bryce walked on with a purposeful stride and forced Leanna to take short, quick steps to keep up with him. Had she hit a nerve that rankled? She let his comment pass.

"Since I've seen The Tug, it's only fitting you see where I'm bunking. Do you have some time?" He gave her a searching look.

Stick to your resolve, a small voice shrieked inside her head. Leanna looked at her watch. The boat would be docked at Chippewa Bay and she could go there and wait until it was time to leave. In her backpack she had a book that would keep her occupied.

"Actually, I have to get back to the boat."

"The boat?"

"The one in which I brought a tourist group."

"I've been meaning to ask you what you were doing here. So that's what's keeping you busy these days."

"That and the store."

He had been so amiable and charming she would have to find a way of leaving that would cause the least amount of friction. Bryce looked puzzled and disappointed when she declined his invitation.

His face hardened. "You have time to take tourists who trample all over the island, scaring away wolves, but no time to see how the study is conducted."

Leanna felt every nerve tighten. "Aren't you presuming too much? For one thing, we haven't seen each other for ions of time. For another, you don't have the right to criticize the tourism that's bringing revenue to the island. You can't expect to have the island turned into a wildlife sanctuary just so you can study wolves." As she felt her spirits sag, Leanna turned away and scanned the horizon.

"Wolves here are at risk. There's been a steady decline to about only fourteen or so on this island since the 1980s." His voice sounded uncompromising, yet oddly gentle.

She would have felt like a heel if she hadn't reminded herself that a workaholic like Bryce would tack on any explanation to justify his vocation.

"It's not about wolves or land or tourism. You're just offended that I won't go along with you. That's what it's been about all those years ago. It's just you all the way." She turned to face him and waited for him to reply. Perhaps she'd said too much. She felt hollow inside. If only she hadn't had these feelings for him still, she could have laughed her way out of his company, joked about their earlier relationship even. But where he was concerned, a cache of emotions had built up and they couldn't be swept away.

"Of course, that's why you ran away without explanation."

"Obviously, it didn't upset you enough to come looking for me."

"If you had wanted me to, I figured you'd have found a way to let me know." He gave her a long look, his gaze still holding her. "Did you want me to chase after you? Were you pregnant, Leanna?"

Bryce's presence affected her the way it always had. But this time it wasn't going to work. Leanna moved away instinctively and insulated herself with physical distance from him. "Don't you think you would've known if I were? I didn't want to tie you down when your work meant everything to you." Leanna held her breath. Would he let it go now? Obviously, he was curious about Kai. She just hoped his curiosity wouldn't go any further.

"So that's it. You were sulking because I didn't want to get married then. And I thought you were different. I thought you'd understand." His tone was civil despite his anger.

Leanna was relieved the querying mood that compelled him to ask about Kai had passed. She couldn't take much more of him hovering around that topic. She needed time to decide when and how she'd tell him about Kai in her own way. It certainly wasn't now, when they were both strangers to each other.

Once she settled the dilemma in her own mind, Bryce's remark caught her on the defensive. "Do you have to be so smug? Don't you know the difference between 'tying the knot' and 'commitment?'" Leanna's face flushed and she pulled away mentally from any tenderness she might have felt. She had taught herself to do that when something upset her.

"I was very involved in my work then. You didn't understand." He turned to her. "What is it, Leanna? What are you looking for?"

"Obviously, not you. And don't bother playing the intrepid psychologist, or maybe that's part of your credentials. Studying wolves leads you to study human beings."

"You'd be surprised how much you learn about people when you study our other co-residents on this planet." He cocked an eyebrow, which she found so comical that she had to suppress a smile.

They hadn't progressed very far on their trek back to where the trail forked, one going deeper into the woods, and the other toward the shops in the clearing.

"I saw that you were involved with your work. That and the fact that I was redundant." Leanna looked him in the eye to challenge him to a verbal duel.

A stony expression descended on his face. Then it vanished, almost as if a memory had resurfaced and he was trying to gain control of its ferocity. "If that's your opinion of things, you're welcome to it." His voice was mellow, almost philosophical.

Surprised at his reaction, she stared at the change that had filtered through his voice and manner. It appeared as if, after so many years of absolute nothingness, two people could still rekindle the embers of their love, given the right moment.

But then another thought intruded. His line of work took him into the woods for too long, and he hadn't seen a female for the longest time, so naturally anything in a skirt, figuratively speaking, was fair game. Well, she wasn't available.

Leanna quickened her step. "Don't let me keep you from your work." She noticed that all he had to do was keep to his usual long strides to maintain his pace and keep her at his side. How infuriating! As usual, he didn't seem to have to make any effort to get what he wanted, however minor.

"You're not." He spoke as one would talk to a sulky, not very bright child. "At the clearing, where you're obviously headed, I take off in another direction toward camp. And contrary to what I've said, I wish you the best in your job as a tourist guide."

"Something you wouldn't understand. People wanting to enjoy the natural beauty of the island." *There I go with the lecturing tone again.*

"Which won't remain beautiful for too long. My colleague, Fred, has been here on wolf studies before and he's seen changes to the island. Changes for the worse."

"Such as?"

"Commercialization. If wolves go, it'll be only a matter of time before birds and other animals start disappearing."

"A one-man champion, aren't you?"

"It can begin with one man."

His Harbor Girl

His quiet pride wasn't lost on her, and she had to admire it as she cast a sideways glance at him. There was no pomposity, only an undercurrent of concern.

She said nothing. She just had to get away from him before the sparks ignited inside herself. Once or twice, she'd caught him glancing at her.

Her thoughts forced her to quicken her steps even more.

"You're in some kind of hurry to get away from me, aren't you?" He moved closer toward her. "I'm not going to compromise your virtue. Isn't that what well-brought-up ladies call it? I haven't the slightest intention of kissing you either. So, you can forget hoping for that." He said the words tentatively, as if testing the idea.

Leanna flushed at his remark, which sounded to her like self-protection. "The audacity of you! I wouldn't kiss you if you were the last person on this planet. I hope I never see you again."

"Really? Then why are your lips pursed like that? Take your compact out of that bag of yours and look at yourself."

"I don't carry compacts."

"Of course. How could I have forgotten that? One of the things I liked about you was your complete indifference to your spectacular looks. And, despite what you might think, it won't upset me too much if I don't see you again either." He tossed out a dry laugh.

Leanna's backpack had been sliding off her shoulder while she walked as fast as she could to keep up with him. With a firm grip she hitched it up again and strode off without a backward glance.

She saw the clearing up ahead and the shops open for business. She decided to browse there in the shops before going to the Chippewa Bay dock.

What was she going to do about Bryce? When she ran into him it was like being sandbagged between the eyes and then being told to ignore it. Still, she'd be able to deal with her predicament—she'd been in tight places before.

Leanna walked on. Bryce's words about "compromising her virtue" whizzed in her ears. There was irony! What would he do if he knew who Kai really was?

She'd promised to bring Kai to the island one day. They were going to hike up and down trails and look for creeks and logs chewed by beavers in their natural enthusiasm for building dams. But then she'd have to face the possibility of Bryce seeing Kai here.

As she entered a shop, her thoughts taunted her like the appearance of a wart on one's hand. She looked through the postcards, but the fun of browsing was interrupted periodically by the persistent drone of Bryce's voice, troubling because she still heard it clearly in her mind and saw that half-mocking expression on his face.

Two hours later, Leanna sat aboard the *Queen* with the distinct feeling she'd escaped. Marcum helped her with her backpack, which had unobtrusively gained weight after she'd wandered though the shops.

"How was your day?"

"Interesting." Leanna's voice was as high-strung as new fishing wire.

* * * *

By the time they made it back to Pelican Harbor she had put Bryce firmly out of her mind. At least, she thought she had.

The next day, being the weekend, customers wove in and out through The Tug. Leanna was kept busy explaining the background of unusual merchandise to some of the customers, and writing up sales slips. She could hear her father in the back fixing a loose floorboard.

"This ornery thing!" he muttered, hammering in nails with short strokes.

She smiled. Her father wasn't happy unless he was fixing something, hammering or sawing or crawling under his truck to check the muffler. He just had to grumble about it first.

Kai wiped the sides of the glass counter and as far as she could reach, which allowed Leanna to help Kai keep her good mood. Her daughter liked "helping Mommy" in the shop.

"Would you like to go to Gramps? Looks like he needs help."

Kai nodded, her face as sober as a middle-aged owl. "And make sure he doesn't hit his thumb." She pronounced it "fumb." She dropped the cloth duster and hurried off with a worried look.

Leanna went through yesterday's sales figures on the computer. They were the same as always. She had taught Chester to record them as they occurred, and he'd give the customers a short printout with a flourish. She saw her father's pride at learning how to use a computer, thanks to her insistence that it would be good for him to learn a new skill.

Customers peered at merchandise in different parts of the store and Leanna felt a sense of mild satisfaction. Roaring success or not, her job was something she liked. At the same time, she stayed around the people she loved—Kai, her father, and now, Alice, who slowly made herself part of the family.

After half an hour or so, Leanna noticed that the hammering had stopped. One more thing had been accomplished. Each day, his arthritis notwithstanding, Chester awoke early and, fortified by several cups of coffee, went about repairing things.

He came into the store with Kai in tow, carrying Chester's hammer.

"I'm helping, Mommy. See?"

"Just want to make sure that nobody trips on loose floorboards. It just wasn't setting as it should." Chester moved over to where Leanna sat near the computer, his hand pressed to his back.

"Is it your back again?"

"Yup. But work goes on. Oh, I forgot to tell you—fellow called Nolan Packard came in askin' for you when you were gone yesterday."

"Nolan Packard? What did he want?"

Leanna's mind drew a quick picture, if a comical one, of the man in a leisure suit and loads of jewelry and an incredible energy for putting up buildings.

"Seems he's thinkin' of doing up a lot of the buildings on the waterfront and asked if we'd ever thought of sprucing up The Tug. I told him the spruced up version is what he's lookin' at and we like it fine the way it is."

Leanna couldn't help smiling at her father's colorful depiction of his conversation with Packard.

But Chester wasn't finished yet. "And I also told him that he should check with you. You're a college-educated gal. You should give him an opinion or two."

"Dad, it's enough if you've told him what you had to. I don't need to see him."

"Don't just dismiss it. See what the man has to say. Besides, seems like there was something else on his mind that he wasn't talkin' about."

"Like what, Dad?" Leanna teased. "Like he wants to buy The Tug for a fortune because he suspects there's buried treasure here?"

His Harbor Girl

Chester shook his head. "Have it your way. Don't say I didn't give my opinion. You put in good money to set up the store."

"Yes, I know. Okay, I'll see Packard and find out what he has to say."

A few days later, when Leanna was just about to close the store, Nolan Packard came in.

"Good afternoon." He looked hot and rumpled in his dark business suit. It had been stifling all day with hardly a rustle breeze lifting off the lake.

He must be the classic example of the aggressive businessman who doesn't dare be caught in a relaxed mode, she thought.

"Lady, you're a hard one to catch." He looked around. "You have a nice place here, as I mentioned to your father."

"Thank you." Leanna stared at the jewel-loaded fingers and the chain around his neck. She had never seen a man wearing so much jewelry. "My father said you wanted to talk to me."

She got up. She knew what he wanted to talk to her about and what her answer would be.

As she watched Packard, an involuntary comparison to Bryce flashed through her mind. Give the man a break. It's not his fault that he doesn't have the pizzazz that Bryce has, or his personality.

"I've invested in property around Pelican Harbor, and I'm giving it a face lift. To keep pace with the rest of the waterfront, I'd like to remodel the outside of your store, for a nominal fee."

Leanna was silent for a few moments. "That's an attractive offer. But I like to pay my own way for any remodeling done here. And, at the moment, I'm not interested in remodeling outside."

"Don't you want to hear what the nominal fee is?" He looked puzzled.

"No, I'm afraid not. Thanks for the offer."

"Then, I'll make another offer. I've put up an apartment building for which I need a manager. I'd like to offer you the job."

"Why me?"

"From what I've heard, you've made a go of this unique store."

Leanna hoped that the store would be viable, but she also needed extra income. She considered his offer; this was one that she could use.

"What do you say?" Nolan asked, and flashed her an encouraging smile.

"I might just take you up on that. I'd like to think it over and let you know in a few days."

Packard smiled. "Fair enough. And I hope we can get to know each other a little better." Leanna did not reply. For her, this was a business proposition, nothing more. She'd have to let him know that before too long. And another thing, maybe this way she could avoid seeing Bryce. Being busy, she'd have to stop taking tourists to the island.

Chapter 4

Leanna closed the file folder marked "Apartment Leases" and locked it away in a steel cabinet next to her desk.

A strong breeze blew in through the window behind her and she basked in its coolness; it had been humid and hot the last several days. She watched the holiday-makers in their colorful summer wear skipping along the beach in the distance, and wished she could do the same.

Ever since she started work at the Lakeview Apartments office, her mind revolved around her work like many-colored glass in a kaleidoscope. Her new job was enough to keep Bryce out of her mind. But every time she looked toward the lake, a question would always pop into her mind like a dart on target. What was Bryce up to?

"How're things going?" Nolan came in with a Cheshire cat grin slowly illuminating his face.

"I had a young couple stop by to look at the apartments, even though there wasn't one vacant. Luckily, Mabel was willing to open up hers. They liked it and asked me to keep them posted if one should come vacant."

As he listened, Nolan seemed to be more interested in staring at her well-fitting pant suit, which made her squirm inside.

"Nolan, are you listening? I thought you would be delighted."

"Of course. Who wouldn't be? To watch you."

"Maybe I should make it clear that this is a 'strictly business' arrangement. For what you're paying me I'll do the job well."

"Of course you will. I have no doubt about that. But can't we be friends too?"

"You mean more than friends." Leanna gave him a cool, level look.

Nolan threw himself into an armchair in the corner of the room.

"You're not seeing anybody, are you?"

"Actually, there is somebody else." There was and wasn't—Bryce.

"Now what do you mean by that?"

"Only that there is somebody."

"Around here? I'm surprised." She saw his eyebrows lift in disbelief.

"Nolan, what does it take for you to get the message?"

"I just don't take 'no' for an answer."

"Have things gone your way all your life?"

"Pretty much."

"You're impossible!"

"Too bad you think so."

"I'm here to do the work. Now, if you'll excuse me, I have to put lease agreements into the computer. Do you want a report or not?" She quelled a surge of annoyance.

He got up and waved both hands. "Go on. Do what you have to do."

Leanna's face broke into a grim smile after Nolan left. She'd given up part of each day managing The Tug for this.

And it wasn't only for the money. She wanted to be part of the development trend that was sweeping Pelican Harbor.

She and Chester were respected members of this community and this was the only town she'd known and loved, except for her stint in college.

Chester had been the classic sailor, always in demand. He had that hail-fellow-well-met quality about him that people liked. Leanna had resented his being away so much, but no one else knew that, except perhaps Alice, with her eagle's eye for people's feelings. She was as sharp as radar for picking up a sensitive spot in others.

Nolan's constant badgering aside, managing the apartments gave Leanna an opportunity to have a pulse on the ebb and flow of people coming and going, and what it meant for her business. Not the least of it was being as close to Kai as possible. Thankfully, she didn't have to go elsewhere to look for work.

Now that Leanna had gotten her life into some semblance of order, she could give Kai more attention. In a few months she'd start kindergarten, a new and wonderful experience for her.

Bryce's presence was like a keg of dynamite in both Leanna's life, and Kai's. She'd come to a cool decision about keeping Bryce out of her life and herself away from him, but how was that all going to work out?

The ear-piercing twang of the phone jostled her hand off the computer keyboard and she reached for the receiver.

"Hello? Dick? What a surprise."

"The *Queen* is making a morning run to the island. I have a woman who's going over to the island."

Leanna wondered what Dick's point was and waited patiently for the rest of the story.

"She's a reporter who's here to interview Bryce Robertson."

Leanna's heart gave a maddening lurch. Bryce was well known in scientific circles and surfaced every now and then on the six o'clock news on the topic of selective breeding in mammals and various other erudite subjects.

"Okay. So?"

"She's got to get to the old Park Service patrol cabin, which is now being used by Robertson and his research group. Thought you could give her directions."

"I could stop over at your office and talk to her."

"You know the ins and outs of the island. That's why I thought of you. Or else, I wouldn't have bothered you."

"Glad to be of help."

Why did you offer to go to the Park Service office? Because I'm helpful. Try again. Because I wanted to see what the woman looks like.

The conversation with herself gave her footsteps a kind of drumbeat like percussion accompaniment as Leanna got into her car and drove off to the Park Service office. *Shame on you,* she thought.

As she drove, she snatched peeps into the rearview mirror and straightened her bangs with her fingers, then messed them up in disgust. Nothing smacked more of insecurity than frequent peeks into the mirror.

When she reached her destination, she saw a blond woman in an expensive-looking pantsuit, carrying a black briefcase as she waited with Dick in the parking lot. Leanna introduced herself.

"Sara Hutchinson. How d'you do?" The woman held a small voice recorder in her hand. "What a nice little place. Out of this world."

Leanna smiled. "Yes, we like it. Are you from a newspaper?"

"*The Environmentalist*, a trade journal. Actually, I've interviewed Mr. Robertson before, but not like this." She nodded her head in the direction of the island. "I need to know how to get there."

"The Park Service patrol cabin is not far from a collection of small shops. Once you get off at Chippewa Bay there are signs posted all around." Leanna could see that Sara had her mind on other things. She seemed more interested in checking the condition of her lipstick. "Follow the signs," Leanna repeated. "Find the shops and you should see the patrol cabin from there."

She turned toward Dick. "I didn't know the patrol cabin was being used." How could she? She'd been too busy trying to escape the very attractive clutches of Bryce Robertson.

"You've met Mr. Robertson?" Sara turned to her in apparent disbelief.

"Yes." Leanna sounded non-committal.

"He is remarkable for his work and talent and extremely bright." Sara sounded awed.

For a hard-boiled female writer for technical journals, Sara Hutchinson seemed enormously moonstruck.

"Does he know you're going over?" Leanna asked.

"I called him a week ago. He may have forgotten by now." Sara gave a nervous giggle.

"Maybe you could give him a call, Dick."

Dick agreed and invited Sara to talk to Bryce.

Leanna had done her bit in cheering Sara on with her assignment. "You're in good hands now," she told Sara.

I must look like a rat caught in a swamp. And here was Sara Hutchinson dressed in a business suit, although totally inappropriate for the safari-like conditions on the island.

The prospect of interviewing Bryce had obviously claimed Sara's interest. She had no more time to waste on Leanna, who couldn't help grinning to herself at Sara's bushy tailed eagerness. It seemed at odds with the raw ambition that leapt out of her otherwise ordinary face.

Glad it's not me. Leanna knew all about ambition and giddy-headed infatuation. *Been there, done that.*

Besides, Sara would keep Bryce busy and out of her way. Wasn't that convenient for her? *Yes,* she told herself with dismal assurance, *it was.*

"Good luck," Leanna said and meant it as she walked out the door.

Back at The Tug, Alice and Kai were minding the store. Kai was brushing her doll's hair with single-minded concentration. Earlier that day, Leanna had promised to take her to Cecily's house and was rewarded with a wide smile and a hug.

Alice's forehead furrowed with concern. "What took you so long? We were worried."

Kai dropped the cloth duster and ran over to get a hug.

"Hello, sweetie." Leanna enveloped Kai in her arms. "Miss me?"

Kai nodded vigorously.

"I stopped at the Park Service office. A reporter who wanted to go over to the island needed directions." Leanna let go of Kai and moved away to put her purse in a cabinet under the counter.

"A reporter?" Leanna understood Alice's query. There hadn't been any of those going over to the island in a long time.

"She's going there to interview Bryce." Leanna tried to ignore the grinding feeling in her stomach. Jealousy?

"Oh?" the word was loaded with meaning.

"Now, Alice, what's on your mind? Spit it out," Leanna said with a laugh. If she knew worrywart Alice, she'd be reading dire consequences into that piece of information right about now.

"A woman with an attractive man like Bryce. All alone on that island. My dear, I don't have to spell it out."

"Alice, when are you going to understand that I no longer carry the torch for Bryce?" To avoid looking up, Leanna sifted through receipts they had taken in sales that morning. She hoped Alice would swallow what she'd just said.

"Is that why you have that mopey look on your face each time somebody mentions his name?"

Leanna did not reply as she felt the crisp pieces of paper crumple under her fingers.

"I'm sorry, I didn't mean to rub it in, but I don't want you getting hurt just when your life is picking up again." The smile faded from Alice's face.

Leanna looked up, her voice light and clear. "You and me both."

Alice moved toward the back where gift boxes had been piled to be put away. She picked up a few then turned around. "By the way, Nolan's really taken a shine to you even though you seem to be ignoring him. And by the look of things, you don't care a penny for him. Must be nice having some man head over heels crazy about you. I'll never know what it's like." She threw the remark over her shoulder and then disappeared into the storage area. Back she came in a few minutes.

Leanna laughed at the mournful look Alice affected for her benefit. "If you mean Dad, keep working on him. I wouldn't give up if I were you. You're good for him."

Alice moved toward the coat hanger and picked up her well-worn sneakers. "Why, thank you. Now, if only he'd think the same. Hand me my purse, will you? I'm off to the supermarket."

"Dad's like a kid in some ways. He needs to be shown what's good for him."

Leanna had seen loneliness in Chester's face, but he'd be the last to admit it. Carpentry kept him busy on most days.

That and his old buddies at the VFW, where they sat around a thick oak table and spun yarns.

"What if Nolan gets serious? Would you marry him?"

"Marry him!" Leanna gave her a quick glance and stashed away sales receipts. "Of all the hare-brained ideas." The thought gave her a sour taste in the mouth.

"Don't knock it, young lady. He's pleasant and rich."

"And I don't love him. You should know better than that. Life isn't always about marrying some rich guy," Leanna said with emphasis.

"I know, I know. Just checking." Alice watched Leanna as if she had deeper concerns she hadn't expressed.

She knew that Alice thought of her as the daughter she never had, hence the nagging, sundry fears.

"Independence is what I want. And that's how it's going to stay." Leanna's voice had a ring of quiet confidence.

"Good for you, girl. And now, I'm really off." Alice hugged Leanna and then shouldered her bag, both in a bear-like gesture.

The day had gone by fast and Leanna prepared to close up shop. She smiled to herself at Alice's oblique tactics in finding out what was on her mind regarding Nolan. Leanna had no doubt that she was rooting for Bryce. As if this were a medieval jousting tournament with Leanna dropping her silken handkerchief onto the tip of the victor's spear. Yet, she couldn't really blame Alice for thinking the way she did.

The back door opened and her father walked in humming tunelessly. One of his singing moods had overcome him.

"In here, Dad. Just closing up."

"How is my Kai-ling?"

"Gramps, what d'you get for me."

"Were you pestering Gramps?" Leanna asked her.

"No, that's what grandfathers are for. Got you a stuffed bunny." He held out a cute little white rabbit.

"Thank you." Kai gave him a hug.

"That's a double treat. She's going over to Cecily's later." Leanna shut off the computer. She was on her way toward the back door when her father spoke again.

"That Robertson guy is going to rent his own plane to get around the island and come here when he wants to."

She turned around. "His own plane?" Her heart beat like a tom-tom drum. Bryce plus plane spelt easy access to the mainland and herself.

"That's what they said at the VFW. They'll be using the spot out by the dock cabin for takeoffs and landings. Guess he figured they couldn't keep waiting for the *Queen* to take 'em back and forth. I hear he goes to Wisconsin a lot."

"He has his research office there, I imagine." As soon as she said it, she felt she shouldn't have popped up with an explanation, when ostensibly, she didn't know much about him.

"There's never been a plane taking off and landing at Pelican Harbor before. There'll be plenty excitement stirrin' up around here."

Leanna nodded. "They're doing wolf population studies."

"Didn't other folks come here and study wolves before?"

"They did, but not with this amount of intensity."

"It'll bring publicity."

"Which isn't all bad." Leanna wondered if Bryce would agree. "Although, some people might say that it might spoil the natural splendor of Pelican Harbor."

"Folks here could use the jobs it might bring to Pelican Harbor," Chester said.

"Bryce mentioned he was concerned about tourists scaring away or doing harm to the wolves."

"When did he say that?"

"I ran into him by chance when I took the tourists there."

Chester gave her a quirky look; his fuzzy eyebrows poised high like furry caterpillars. "Interesting."

"What?"

"That you ran into that fella. Seems like he knows his stuff." Chester sounded impressed. "Sure to go far, too."

"What are you really trying to say, Dad? That I should try to get to know him better maybe?" She tensed, waiting for his reply.

"No, nothing like that. But you sure seem lonely sometimes."

"Funny, I thought the same about you."

"Did you, now? Stop worrying. I'm fine. Besides, nobody could replace your mother."

Leanna glanced at Kai, fidgeting with the back door with a child's typical impatience so that it twanged like an improvised wind instrument.

"You surprise me, Dad. You weren't home a lot when she was alive." She tried to keep bitterness out of her voice.

"You think I don't realize that every day?"

"I'm sorry. I know you do." Warmth and sympathy surged through her, and she felt the pain her tired old father must have experienced, first when he realized his shortcomings, and then, when her mother died. Still, that didn't alleviate the hurt of bygone days.

She gave him a hug. "I've got to go before Kai breaks the door."

Chester laughed. "Goodnight, Lea. You've always been a good kid. And now you're a good mother."

Leanna stepped out into the blazing sunset-filled air, feeling curiously soothed. It was the first time she had been able to reach out to her father long enough to detect the hurt he carried around. She had assumed he didn't have any.

* * * *

Bryce kept his eyes peeled when Kip LaSalle circled the small Piper Cub aircraft around a wolf pack several times until his head roiled from the dizzying aerobatics that Kip performed.

"Go easy, will you? I'd like to hang on to my breakfast." Bryce had his head half out of the window with a hand on his camera's telephoto lens.

"How do the pictures look? I can get closer." Ever the intrepid pilot, Kip winged even lower, making smaller and smaller circles with each pass.

Bryce's camera snapped noisily as he took several frames in rapid succession. "You can tell the camera's quality by the amount of noise it makes." When he was finished he sat back and let out a sigh of relief.

"Easy, Bryce. Relax; I've been flying close to fifteen years. You have nothing to fear." Kip surveyed his boss with a grin. "Did I ever tell you about the time I lost one engine and had to bail out?"

"Please, Kip." Bryce hid his alarm with a poker face. "I'm sure you did fine then. But for now, just get us back to the ground."

Kip chuckled, as if enjoying the whole thing. "You got it. You finished with the count?"

"No, not yet. Just go easy on the rollovers."

Bryce had gotten pictures of a wolf pack on a new kill in a cedar swamp, thanks to some landmarks that Kip had previously located. The next time, Kip could probably bring the plane around in a tight turn so Bryce could get a closer look for more pictures.

Kip had taught Bryce everything he needed to know to locate wolves from the aircraft. They had been together at previous aerial surveys in Minnesota and other states. Kip's ability to follow wolf tracks was indispensable to Bryce and his research group. Kip did this by simply turning the plane on its side and circling tightly, all the while watching for subtle clues on the ground.

Several close passes later, Bryce was satisfied with the pictures he'd taken and decided it was time to descend. He made a count of the wolves he'd seen, associating the wolves with familiar landmarks to return to them. Obviously, a den stood somewhere nearby, judging by all the wolf tracks he'd seen.

"Okay. Haul away."

"Aw, just when I was enjoying it."

"There'll be other times."

"If you promise."

Bryce grinned at Kip's enthusiasm. He was fearless and a little crazy at times. And, most likely, born in the cockpit of an aircraft.

No sooner had Bryce given the word than Kip climbed to a comfortable altitude. When they reached their cabin location, he brought the plane down smoothly.

"How's that?" Kip asked.

"Perfect landing."

"Good old retractable landing gear. No extra charge, either."

His Harbor Girl

"Can't thank you enough, Kip," Bryce said, entering the cabin. "Excuse the cramped living quarters. Hope you don't mind sharing with Fred and me."

"That's all right. I know when I get back to civilization I can more than make up for all this." He waved his hand about the cabin.

To Bryce, Kip looked like a pirate with his cap on backwards and an earring in one ear. But he had a sharp eye for wolf tracks and a sturdy constitution.

Bryce pushed aside a stack of computer printouts and laid his camera bag on the table. He emptied the camera and stored the film roll in a canister he'd found in his duffel bag. He had two more canisters of films to be processed.

"I'll need you to take these to the Wisconsin lab, Kip."

"Sure thing. If you don't need me here the next few days, I'll take a run up that way tomorrow."

"Any excuse to get into that flying saucer of yours, huh?" Bryce grinned at him.

At that moment, Fred came in with a loping walk. "You back?"

Bryce nodded. "All in one piece. Where were you?"

"In the storage shed, measuring the wolf specimen we found yesterday. Don't worry, I used gloves and had a wash and scrub up there." He held up his forearms in mock-surgeon fashion.

"All right. I buy that." Bryce resumed examining his camera.

"So how was the...interview...with that woman reporter?" The insinuating glint in his eye spoke volumes.

"She's from *The Environmentalist*, and has interviewed me before."

"Lucky she caught us during our browse study. She'd have walked right past us if we hadn't come out of the woods behind the patrol cabin."

"The dry log outside made a good bench to be interviewed on," Bryce said.

"She's a babe."

"Is she?" Bryce hadn't noticed. "She's all yours."

"Thanks, partner, but as long as you're around, she won't notice me."

"Don't worry, I won't spoil it for you," Bryce said with deliberate nonchalance. The only woman he wanted to notice him seemed to be avoiding him like the plague. The picture in his mind was that of Leanna's tantalizing face and thick, dark hair, cascading to the shoulders, not that of a pushy, blond reporter.

The whole time he had been in the plane during the aerial tracking, he'd wished Leanna had been with him enjoying the view. He had a rare feeling of conquest and elation when looking down despite the illusion of danger, which Kip did everything to foster. Darn his troublesome antics!

"She'll be ba-a-ack," Fred said in a singsong voice. "She's set her cap for you, buddy."

"Tell you what," Bryce said. "If she does return, I'll suggest that she interview you. After all, you're my associate."

"Bathing in your glory. You're the big name in this business."

"No, I'm not. And there are no 'big names' in preserving wildlife. We're all pulling together."

Fred patted him on the back. "You're an okay guy, you know."

Bryce grinned. Fred was just an overgrown kid. "Coming from you, that's a whopping big compliment."

His Harbor Girl

It had been several weeks since Bryce had seen Leanna standing there amidst copper artifacts, glass ornaments and agate jewelry of her store. He went to the cabinet in the kitchen area and, opening it, peered inside. The cans of food were dwindling. He could send Kip to fetch supplies from Pelican Harbor, but it wasn't right to send him for food supplies.

He was strictly there for aerial surveys and emergencies. Bryce would have to thumb a ride with him to Pelican Harbor to pick up supplies.

His breath hitched. He had just figured out a way to see Leanna without causing the least bit of suspicion. He looked at Fred, who sat staring at the logbook. He made entries as soon as he completed a job. Bryce had impressed upon him the necessity of noting the time, the atmospheric temperature, and the conditions under which a specimen had been found.

"We're running out of supplies," Bryce said. "Of course, I can always get them from the only food supply store at the island."

"Are you crazy?" Fred nearly had apoplexy. "The stores here ask for a pound of flesh along with your money."

"You're so right. I'd better go to Pelican Harbor. Kip?"

"Say no more, boss. Just let me know when, and I'll take you there."

Bryce hadn't decided. He just wanted to know that if he wanted to he could see Leanna. But first, he had his own entries to make, entries about where he'd taken the pictures, if the wolves were in packs or if they were strays, the altitude at which they had been flying. He took out a ledger-type hard cover book and started jotting notes, which he would later put in the computer.

He glanced at Fred, busy scribbling away in his log book and grinned to himself. He could be trouble if he chose, kidding him about going across to the Harbor. Fred had to read momentous meanings in everything Bryce did that didn't have to do with wolf tracking.

"What speed were we flying?" Bryce looked at Kip. He had been so busy hanging on to his camera, his breakfast, and sometimes, dear life itself, that he had neglected to check the instrument panel.

"Ninety miles an hour."

"And how long does the fuel last?"

"About two and a half hours."

"Good. That's plenty."

"Wait till the weather gets bad."

"And then what happens."

"We have to remember the direction of the cabin," Kip said with blatant complacency.

"Sorry I asked." Bryce returned to his entries.

* * * *

Bryce sat back in his seat as the Piper soared over Lake Superior and headed toward Pelican Harbor. No camera to wield today, or wolf tracks to observe, just the crystal blue of lake and sky. And the prospect of seeing Leanna's round-eyed surprise when he walked through the door to pick up his supplies. Would she be pleased to see him this time? The once beckoning look in her eyes had vanished in the years they'd lost touch with one another. He had sensed cold disillusionment in them even though she'd spoken to him in a soft voice. It must have been hard to raise a child on her own. Well, he could change all that. Not overtly; he was more subtle than that. Maybe he could put the light back in her eyes.

"You're very quiet, boss," Kip said, glancing at Bryce out of the corner of his eye. "I'm not even doing any flips. What's on your mind?"

"Just making a mental note of the things I need to get. Thanks for dropping off the films at the Wisconsin lab."

"Sure. I'll have to get more fuel, anchor rope and such. We'll be landing near the dock cabin. Okay by you?"

Bryce nodded, then strained to look out the cabin window. "Our jeep is parked there. I'll be using that to get around."

In a short while, Kip touched down on the blacktopped landing area. He tipped his index finger in a playful salute as Bryce ducked and rushed toward the Park Service parking lot.

Minutes later, Bryce ran lightly up the steps and pulled open the door of The Tug. Leanna would soon look up from her computer and there he would be standing in front of her. This time he hoped she'd look up with delight instead of the blanched look he had gotten the last time.

The bell overhead tinkled as he walked in. His gaze sought the counter where he'd seen Leanna last time and he stood frozen for a moment.

"May I help you?" It was one of the elderly ladies he'd held open the door for last time. "Oh, it's you, Mr. Robertson. How are you?" She pushed aside a cardboard box on the counter. "You and your men have been so quiet over at the island that we'd all been wondering what you were up to."

"Actually, we've been busy tracking wolves," Bryce replied with a grin. He ignored the impatient thud in his chest. "Is...er...Leanna here?"

"No, she works part of the day managing apartments." With annoying deliberation Alice started taking out small shell-like objects by the handful. She seemed determined not to say anything more and just keep him swallowing his impatience.

"Really?" Bryce gave her a bright smile which caused her to abandon her work and gape at him. "Which apartments?"

He picked up a postcard with studied carelessness and put it back.

"The new Lakeview Apartments, a mile up toward town. They belong to Nolan Packard. He owns several buildings around Pelican Harbor."

Yes, he'd heard the name. Leanna worked for him? Or maybe it was more than work. She was free, after all, to have relationships where she chose, and his showing up here probably wouldn't change that. He felt his jaw clench despite the rational explanation he'd just given himself. He had an idea of what he was going to do now.

"I came to get supplies."

"Please go right ahead. And if you need any help, call me."

Bryce picked up nonperishable items. He needed those for munching while pondering his notes at the end of the day. He also found a plastic bucket for soaking clothes in, writing pads, and a few other things. After paying for the items, he picked up the bag and turned to leave.

"Would you like me to tell Leanna you stopped by?" Alice asked, walking him to the door.

"No, that's all right, thanks."

Bryce strode out to the jeep, hopped in and turned the key in the ignition, his mouth setting in a determined line. He'd come to see Leanna. So help him, he would.

Chapter 5

Bryce glanced at his watch. Eleven forty-five. He maneuvered the winding road that led up to Lakeview Apartments, parked, and studied the white apartment building. He wondered if he should go up to the manager's office or wait in the parking lot, then decided not to disturb Leanna at work. Maybe he could just fill his lungs with the balmy air and watch the seagulls zigzagging and screeching in sync. What would she be doing at this very moment? He felt himself tense with anticipation.

* * * *

Leanna opened the desk drawer and pulled out her purse. It was time to lock up and leave. It had been a busy day, showing prospective tenants around and taking phone calls from out of town people, some of whom wanted an apartment just for the summer and fall. And then, thoughts of Bryce filtered into her mind, making a tough day worse. She clutched her purse and stepped into the corridor, her pencil skirt forcing her to take shorter steps. Pleased with the day's work, she looked forward to spending the afternoon with Kai and relieving Alice at The Tug.

A warm breeze fanned her face as she stepped outside and the large entrance doors swung behind her. On the way to her station wagon, she caught a hazy glimpse of a gray jeep parked at a distance. Bryce's tall, languid figure leaned against it, watching her, and the corners of his mouth turned upward in a half-smile. A flicker of apprehension coursed through her. She wouldn't allow herself to believe he was looking for her, so it had to be one of his colleagues he sought.

"About time," he said, sounding cheerful.

"What are you doing here?" Edginess laced her voice.

"The day is perfect for a picnic. However, I'll settle for taking you to lunch."

Leanna stopped an arm's length in front of him. She could feel his closeness like a blazing surge of electricity. She sucked in her breath and steeled herself against the hypnotic spell he wove over her right out of the blue.

"Lunch?" Fear knotted inside her. She had to pick up Kai from morning daycare, and there was no telling what he might think when he saw her. "I'm afraid I can't."

"Oh? May I ask why?"

"Because I have to pick up Kai from daycare."

"Kai?"

"My daughter."

Leanna looked directly at his piercing gray eyes as she spoke, but she saw no reaction to her mention of Kai. She felt herself go slack with relief.

"Too bad." He swung himself into the driver's seat of his jeep. "I'd have loved to take the two of you to lunch. Does your daughter look like you?"

An innocent enough question but to her nervous way of thinking there seemed to be a hint of suspicion in it. Added to that, a curious expression showed on his face, one that asked a million questions.

"You didn't tell me you were ever married." His hand rested lightly on the steering wheel and he looked up at her in a slow, sweeping gaze.

Leanna swallowed the lump in her throat and avoided his gaze. "I wasn't."

"I see." His voice was low and controlled. A long pause followed and she counted the seconds silently.

"If you'll excuse me." Leanna started to get into her car, unable to shake off the effect of his proximity and her own waning poise.

She turned the key in the ignition. But no reassuring roar of the engine shook the vehicle. Giving the key some slack she turned it again. This time, the engine croaked like a jaded frog. No, not now, she thought, it can't be dead. The station wagon had seen many cold harsh winters, left outside without a garage. Now, when she needed to get away from Bryce, it sat lifeless like a once-active volcano that had run out of lava.

She sighed and sat for a few seconds, her hand folded over the bunch of keys. A knock on the window forced her to turn around, and she got an eyeful of Bryce grinning at her. In past years, she'd melt like butter at that grin. But not now.

"You need a ride somewhere?"

She nodded, feeling defeated. She couldn't sit here forever, so why balk at it? Better go and pick up Kai before she started crying, wondering why her mother didn't come. She just prayed that Bryce wouldn't look too closely at Kai and see himself in her as Alice did. If only she could leave him there and walk off.

Leanna got out of her car and followed him to the jeep. They pulled out of the parking lot and waited at the entrance to the road for a break in the traffic.

"Turn into the main road and go straight. I'll tell you when to take a left turn." She cast him a sidelong glance. The wind blew in through the open windows, flopping his thick hair over his forehead. A faint smile played on his face as he concentrated on the road and she couldn't tear her gaze away from that face.

"How's business been at The Tug?"

"Good." How strange it seemed to be sitting next to the man about whom she'd been crazy all those years ago. What did she feel now? Hardened, she decided. Years of bringing up Kai alone had drained her emotions of their juices. But now, an electrifying palpitation at the sight of Bryce took hold of her. He looked so different that he hardly resembled the absent-minded doctoral student she used to know. It was more than his physical appearance. He had a mature look that drew her to him, and she wondered if he felt the same toward her, or if this would be another time in her life when her emotions were stronger than his. She wouldn't let herself be hurt again. Somehow she'd find the strength and keep an emotional distance between herself and Bryce until she finally got out of this situation today.

"The store has been good for all of us." She didn't want to mention how much Kai had enriched her life. Kai was a precious commodity she wanted to keep to herself.

"You'll have to tell me where to turn."

The business district disappeared and they passed a church and the public library.

"There it is. My Buddy and Me."

Bryce turned deftly into an ungenerous parking spot left by two cars parked at an awkward angle.

"Thank you. You don't have to wait."

"How will you get back?"

"A friend can pick me up." A split second later, Leanna realized the thoughtlessness of that statement. Bryce picked up on it.

"So I'm not a friend. Okay, maybe I deserved that."

"No, I meant…"

He held up his hands. "It's all right. What will you do with your car?"

"I'll have the service garage pick it up and repair it. It probably needs a new battery."

"In the meantime." Bryce unlocked his seatbelt and opened the door. "I'll be your chauffeur."

Leanna paused to reconsider but her mind was too sluggish to study the pros and cons. She had no other alternative at the moment. "I'll accept your offer to drive us home, but no more."

She opened her door and got out just in time to hear the bell ring; the morning session was over. Through the bright orange front door, the children came out, chattering and clutching colorful school bags. Kai headed the group, her hair flying in the wind as she ran toward Leanna.

"Mommy!"

Leanna bent down and gave her a hug. "Hi, sweetie."

Kai stopped fidgeting and stared at the tall man standing next to her mother.

"This is Bryce."

Kai went on staring, her brown eyes wide with a child's curiosity. Finally, she seemed to relent and let go of her silent appraisal of him. "He-lo."

"Hello, Kai. Can I shake your hand?" Bryce knelt down and took her hand in his.

Kai shook his hand solemnly, causing Leanna to smile. Then she looked up at Leanna. "Can we go to Red Barn, Mommy?"

"May I take you two lovely ladies to lunch?" Bryce's charm flowed freely. But Leanna sensed a ring of sincerity in his voice. For some reason, he wasn't going to let them go without taking them to lunch. Perhaps he wanted to observe Kai. The thought caused a sudden chill to grip her heart.

Leanna smiled at him, not wanting to give away her thoughts. "Oh, all right. Thank you. Looks like Kai is ravenous. Maybe we'd better go and eat lunch."

"Good. Where would you like to go?"

"Red Barn is just down the road." Leanna had often taken Kai there.

Bryce followed Leanna and Kai toward the jeep and opened the back door for Kai. "In you go. Let me help you with your seatbelt."

After buckling her in, he opened the front passenger door for Leanna.

"Red Barn it is." With a light-hearted chuckle, Bryce started the engine. They drove down the quiet street to a small restaurant that looked like a cozy old barn painted brick red with a brown roof. A miniature haystack stood by the side of it, and a yellow plastic slide for kids adjacent to a swing set completed the play ensemble. There was outside dining so customers could bring their food outside and enjoy it while watching the children play.

Bryce parked the jeep. Leanna helped Kai out and looked for a table.

"If you give me your orders I'll go in and get the food while you grab a table. No sense in all of us going in. It's nice outside. What would you like, Kai?"

"Drumsticks and mashed potatoes, please."

Bryce looked at Leanna, his eyebrows raised in a question.

"Drumsticks, roll and coffee. And a small carton of milk for Kai."

Leanna led Kai to a table with a pink and white gingham cover held down by a small painted rock. Kai sat on the white stool and looked around her happily.

"Hungry?" Leanna smiled at Kai. She slung her purse on the hand-rest of her chair, leaned back and looked up. A breeze blew white cloud bundles across the sky and she breathed in the fresh, cool air. Of all the crazy things, having lunch with Bryce after these many years. Things were different now, like a date with a stranger that Bruce had become to her. They couldn't simply pick up where they'd left off.

Bryce came out bearing a tray piled with food. "Come and get it," he said in an imitation of Daffy Duck, which Kai found very funny and burst out laughing. "I knew you'd like that," Bryce said, setting the drumsticks on a small paper plate for Kai. "And here's your milk."

Leanna watched dreamily. So this was how he'd look as a father if he weren't so averse to making a commitment. She was tormented by confusing emotions for a few moments, until finally, she realized that she was the one who left.

"What did you do in school today?"

"We grew little seeds."

"Grew little seeds?"

"Planted them in little paper cups." Kai made a picture of a cup with her chubby little hands.

Bryce looked interested. "They'll grow into nice plants, I bet. Is your drumstick good?"

Kai nodded, licking her fingers.

Leanna listened to their exchanges trying to keep her eyes on her meal. What effortless ease he had with Kai! A twinge of jealousy ripped through her. How easy for him to show up one day and charm their daughter while she had spent the last few years worrying about her, protecting her from fever and bruises.

"Mommy, can I go play on the slide?"

"Yes, if you're finished. Wipe your hands."

Excited, Kai wiped her hands and ran off to the play area.

"She's full of energy." Leanna's eyes softened as she watched Kai's retreating figure.

"You've been quiet all through lunch." Bryce held her with his gaze.

"I'm sorry. I didn't mean to." Leanna tried to look cheerful. She had given away her mood too easily. "Kai likes you."

"She's a great kid." Bryce's voice was soft, contemplative.

"I'm lucky. I've had my difficult moments." She said that just to let him know it wasn't easy bringing up a child. Rib-breaking jealousy about sharing Kai with Bryce made her watch her words.

"I never guessed you had a daughter. You didn't say anything when I saw you at the store that first day."

"There was no need to bother you with the events in my life." Leanna made sure her words had just the right touch of informality and toughness.

"Sorry I mentioned it." Bryce looked away into the distance. Maybe he was thinking she'd lay open her life's history for him so he'd feel compassion for her. Men ran at the first sign of emotion. Only she'd run first, a sort of reverse precaution against him letting her down again.

"Still, you can't blame me for saying it, Leanna. After all, we were in love once. If Kai were our child, you wouldn't have left. At least, I'm assuming you wouldn't." His eyebrows lifted in a question, his gray eyes growing darker, like the sky giving the hint of an approaching storm. He rested his elbows on the table and studied her.

"It won't do you any good to look at me like that. I'm not the girl you used to know." Leanna swallowed hard, lifted her chin, and boldly met his gaze.

"I'm finding out." A quiet assurance came through in his voice. "This Packard fellow. How much do you know about him?"

"Enough to take the job he offered. What does it matter to you, anyway?"

"Gossip is that he's pushy enough to get whatever he wants."

"That has nothing to do with me."

"You sure?"

"You don't know the half of it, Bryce." She permitted herself a withering stare; she didn't care for the suspicions he had just voiced. They were the insinuations of a man toward his lover, but she and Bryce weren't in that mode now, so why did it matter to him who she worked with?

His voice, though quiet, now held an overtone of coldness. "It *was* another man, wasn't it? And you were pregnant, which was why you ran away without even a hint to me."

He sounded curt, abstracted. His lips were a thin line, jaws clenched. Leanna followed his gaze to where Kai still played on the pale mauve swing set, her feet touching the ground and kicking off as she swung. How could he even accept the fact that there might have been another man in her life when she'd been head over heels in love with him?

"You want answers after all these years?" She laughed to cover her annoyance.

He stiffened as though she had struck him. "It's not a matter of picking up and searching for somebody who's run off without a word. I had my life and work. When my research brought me here I decided to combine it with my search for you. What a waste of energy that's been, seeing that you have a different life now." He paused. "No matter what the circumstances, Kai is a great kid. Don't get me wrong on that."

"Some love. You waited until your work brought you here." Leanna let out a weary sigh.

"You just expected me to run after you because you decided to leave?"

"I see there's no point in talking to you. I'd like to go home, please."

They stared at each other through a ringing silence. Leanna turned away, picked up her plate and Kai's, and stuffed them in the trash bin nearby.

Bryce stood up, his expression incomprehensible. "Suits me." He waited for her to fetch Kai, who looked content to leave.

Leanna helped Kai into the back of the jeep as Bryce watched, looking grim. She tried to hide her inner misery from his probing stare, furious at her vulnerability to him. His coldness stunned her. Served her right for accepting a ride from him and thinking things could even appear normal between them. There was just too much history, too many hurts to overcome. Some that, in all fairness, Bryce knew nothing about. Yet, they stood between them like an impenetrable brick wall.

They sat without a word spoken between them as he drove. Kai chattered on like a magpie, oblivious to the lack of conversation of the grownups. "The slide was fun. I had a friend to play with too. I like drumsticks." She went on in the scattered logic of a child of her age. "Can we go back there again, Mommy?"

"Huh? Yes, yes." Leanna's gaze drifted out to the coolness of the green and the shade cast by the maples they passed, but she was conscious of Bryce sitting only an arm's length away. What followed had the effect of cold water poured over her.

"Are you coming over to my house?" Kai said to Bryce.

Leanna sat in stunned silence and waited for his reply.

"I'd love to, but I'm not sure your Mommy wants me there. So let's make it another day, huh?"

There was a smile in his voice even though Leanna wasn't about to turn and look at him.

"We have to go to the shop and relieve Aunty Alice," Leanna reminded her daughter. "Besides, don't you want to help me at the store?"

"Yeah, I guess."

"Aren't you sure?" Leanna knew Kai would never forfeit the importance she felt when called upon to help out at the shop. No doubt, it was Bryce and his charming personality that made Kai forget about The Tug.

"I'll come again. Now I have to get back to the island." Bryce's voice had the reassuring ring so endearing to very young children.

"The island? We're going to the island, too, right, Mommy?"

Leanna tried to keep calm while her face felt hot and flushed by the effort of having to keep Kai and Bryce at two opposite ends of a pole. She didn't want the two of them getting too friendly even though she didn't really know why. She'd been fine until he showed up.

"One of these days. Promise."

They neared the lakefront.

"Where do you want me to drop you?" Bryce asked. It was the first time he'd spoken to her since their argument.

"At my house. The road that goes up from behind The Tug leads to a row of houses. I need to check on Cody and take him along to the shop."

"Cody? You still have him?" He glanced at her in utter disbelief.

"Yes. He's a big boy now."

"I see." Bryce's wide-eyed astonishment vanished and he reverted to stony-faced preoccupation.

Driving up the hill toward a colorful assortment of houses, he said. "Do you like managing the apartment building?"

"Yes." Her voice seemed to come from a long way off. "I do it for extra funds. The Tug doesn't bring in as much as I'd hoped. Someday, I'd like to build a snack bar to attract tourists who come for hiking in the fall and skiing in the winter."

The next minute she regretted the casual confession of her dream. It wasn't his business and she had no intention of parading her financial problems in front of him.

"Really?" he replied without inflection. "Looks like Nolan Packard showed up like a timely lifeline."

Leanna jerked around to face him, stunned by his bluntness. In the backseat Kai talked to herself, pretending to be the teacher at her daycare. She was oblivious to the tension between her mother and Bryce, Leanna noted with relief. "Save your caustic remarks. You have suspicion written all over your face."

"Can you blame me? After what you did?" His curt voice lashed at her.

"What *did* I do? Leave without telling you when things weren't going anywhere between us." She glared at him with burning, reproachful eyes. "I don't owe you any explanations for why I left, if that's what you're thinking. Especially since you're incapable of trust."

Leanna held her breath, waiting for the road to turn toward the driveway of her house. There at the window stood Cody, his tail wagging like pussy willows in a gale. From the chatter in the back seat, Leanna gathered that Kai couldn't wait to go home and tell Cody all about her adventures today.

"Do you want to pet my dog?" Kai asked Bryce shyly as he parked the jeep.

"I'd love to but I have to go." He got out of the jeep and waited for Kai to scramble out. Bending toward her, he lowered his voice. "Tell you what. When I come again, I'll bring him a treat. Think Cody would like that?"

"Oh, yes. Mommy, can Bryce come on a picnic with me and you and Cody and Grampa and..."

"We'll see, sweetie. Here's the key. Now run along and let Cody out so he can do his business."

Kai skipped away happily toward the house, ignoring Leanna and Bryce, who now glared at each other like combatants ready to pick up arms again.

Bryce kicked a stone near his foot. "You seem to forget that, in the end, I did come looking for you."

"After I started a new life? What did you expect to find?"

"Honest answers," he snapped.

"I've given you the only answers you need, Bryce." Leanna threw the words at him like stones being tumbled in a quarry.

"All right." He glowered at her and turned away. "I was right. When I started out to come here, I hoped to find something of the girl I used to know. But I see she's gone."

A sudden chill hung on the edge of his words and Leanna sensed his anger. The fact that he spoke the truth stung her. She swallowed hard. How soon the cheery tenor of their afternoon together had turned into a contest of opposing memories filled with recriminations. Too much had happened to both of them to try and grasp the gossamer thread of young love. Still, he'd come to look for her, or so he said. Mixed feelings zapped through and she tried to control them.

"Yes, Bryce, it's not meant to be. That's the wisest thing you've said so far."

She bit her lip and looked away, suddenly anxious to escape any more revelations she might unconsciously make. She didn't want to turn into a shrew. She only wanted to state her case and couldn't help it if some of the frustrations of her loneliness came to the surface.

As Leanna turned to go inside, Cody came trotting out at full tilt and headed straight for Bryce whose eyebrows shot up in surprise. "Whoa, Cody."

Unfazed he bent down and extended a hand, letting Cody sniff it. He made a circle around Bryce, squatted in front of him and wagged his tail furiously, to Leanna's annoyance. That was Cody's way of enticing somebody to play with him. Now Bryce had her dog in thrall.

"Cody, come back here!" Leanna called out sharply from the door of her house. But the energetic dog went right on enjoying Bryce's friendly pats on the head as he talked to Cody all the while.

Leanna stood with arms crossed and tapped her foot with the scolding impatience of a metronome. Now she'd have to rescue Cody from Bryce's coaxing manner that knew no boundary with children or animals. Was there anyone who could resist that special sparkle of his? It had gotten her into the predicament she found herself in years ago. Now, when she wanted to get him off her yard, she couldn't manage it.

Kai was inside, probably foraging for cookies, or she'd be out here joining Cody in the Bryce for Hero-of-the-Hour Campaign.

A sigh escaped her as she waited for her dog to quit flattering Bryce and vice versa. This had to stop. She strode out to where Bryce now rolled on the grass with Cody licking his face.

"Do you mind? I have to take Cody inside. It's his lunch time." Restless and irritable as she was, Leanna held herself back from saying anything more.

"Okay, Cody, enough face time. Your mama wants you home." Bryce got up and dusted himself off.

Blades of grass stuck to his thick hair. Leanna fought back an incredible urge to brush them off. Annoyed with herself at the quicksilver changes in her feelings she said, "Here, Cody. Inside, boy."

Ever the obedient mama's boy, Cody, subdued, trotted back into the house with a last backward glance at Bryce.

The moment Cody left, Bryce's lips puckered in annoyance. "Afraid that Cody might like me too?" he drawled with distinct mockery.

"I have to hand it to you. You have a way with dogs and kids." She couldn't ignore the twinge of envy.

His eyebrow quirked up. "I believe that's a compliment! It's only you I haven't been able to win over."

If only that were true she'd be safe and heart-whole, but she wouldn't give him the satisfaction of knowing that. "There are some things you have to earn."

"Believe me, I mean to try. I'm not one to give up."

"Quit before someone gets hurt. I'm a different person now."

"True, but there's got to be something of the girl I once knew. Even you can't have changed all that much." He strode to the jeep, his long lean body moving with the grace of a jaguar.

Did he know his own power? Leanna suspected he did. It showed in his carriage and in the pride dormant in those chiseled features. The next moment he jumped into the jeep and was gone.

Leanna went inside and shut the door. Then she moved to the window and watched him pull out of the driveway faster than the speed limit would allow at Dylan Heights, a tidy little residential area overlooking a bluff.

As the jeep wound out of sight she tried to keep her fragile control. What would his presence at Benedict Island do to her and Kai? She hardly cared to think about that, especially if Bryce had any suspicion that Kai was his daughter.

She sighed and moved away from the window. Her fears were premature. He'd see the settled quality of her life. No need for him to know about Kai, if Leanna didn't tell him. And she didn't plan to unless the situation warranted it.

Cody peeked at her from behind the door leading to the kitchen.

"Hungry? You've been such a good boy," Leanna said. Except when he fell all over Bryce so shamelessly.

Cody sat on his haunches, head angled to one side, tongue hanging out, so that his face assumed a smiling expression. He trotted toward the narrow closet that contained dry dog food, sat in front of it and wagged his tail, as if he were cheering her on in her chores.

She laughed. "All right, all right. I'm getting there."

"Cody, know what I did? I played on the swing and the slide," Kai called out from behind, her hands over her mouth. Her mouth full of chocolate chip cookies made her cheeks bulge like a chipmunk's.

Leanna turned around. "Kai did you finish up all the cookies I made yesterday?" She tried to look stern as she placed Cody's dish in front of him. But she only succeeded in suppressing a chuckle. Kai looked so comical.

"No, Mommy. 'Course not."

"When Cody's done eating, we'll have to go to The Tug. Aunty Alice will need to go home. First, I'd better call the service garage and have my car towed away and fixed. There go another few hundred dollars."

Kai's eyebrows puckered in a look of anxiety. "Are we poor, Mommy?"

"No, just broke."

Leanna picked up the phone and dialed Superior Transmission and explained that her car wouldn't start. No problem, the owner assured her. They would take care of it and give her a good deal on it. Chester had done him a favor and now it was his turn to return it.

She replaced the receiver and a warm feeling surged through her. This had been the only thing that went right today.

An hour later, a small crew consisting of Leanna, Kai and Cody headed out to The Tug. Leanna trudged on, holding Cody's leash in one hand and Kai's little hand clutched in her other one.

The late afternoon brought in a breeze off the lake, which looked like bright blue glass in the distance. Yet, the beauty of the vibrant day failed to invigorate her. All she could see in her mind's eye was the stony mask that Bryce's face had assumed after lunch. The memory of it left her with an emptiness echoing inside. Yet, what had she expected? That he would be overjoyed at finding her with a daughter?

Leanna shook back her wayward hair and her hand tightened on the leash. She'd come this far and she wouldn't let Bryce intimidate her or make her feel guilty.

They climbed down the side of the rolling hill, using a track that led to the back entrance of The Tug.

Leanna looked toward the parking space at the back. "I don't see Grampa's pickup there. Maybe he's taken a run into town." Her gaze scanned the side of Chester's apartment where he had started building a patio the size of a small pen.

"So you girls can sit when the weather is nice," he'd said. "Er…you too, Alice." The afterthought made Leanna suspect that he had Alice in mind mostly, and she had grinned at her father's roundabout way of approaching the topic.

"Hello, anybody home?" Leanna called out as she entered with Cody and Kai in tow.

"In here, honey." White square-shaped boxes that she had stacked up to throw away surrounded Alice. "Your father's gone into town to pick up plywood, and we need to move these ceramic vases. They're getting crowded here and don't show well."

Leanna laughed. "I see you've been busy."

"Where have you been?"

"My car refused to start. Battery's dead. So Bryce gave me a ride to the daycare. Then we had lunch and after that, he dropped us off at home." Leanna's eyes gleamed wickedly as she watched Alice's stare.

"Okay. But did anything interesting happen? How did you run into Bryce?" Alice's forehead creased into deep ruts. "Wait, now I remember. He came in here expecting to see you."

"Really?" Leanna made sure she sounded casual.

"He looked disappointed to see me. Don't worry, that's the effect I have on all men. All except Gerry, God rest his soul." Alice smiled benignly. "Then Bryce bought some things and left."

"I met him at the parking lot after work."

It was a cinch Bryce had planned it that way. She didn't know whether to feel flattered or scared. Obviously he just wanted a fling, someone to pass the time with while he stayed on the island. He claimed he was looking for her, but the question was why? To hash over the past, or just to have a good time for the few months he'd be stuck here?

"Waiting for you, was he?" Alice's hands were busy sorting but her eyes threw Leanna a profound look as she said with a sigh, "Ah, young love."

"Oh, knock it off," Leanna said. She didn't feel the least bit romantic after the altercation with Bryce.

"Suit yourself." Alice sounded resigned.

"We have too many differences now. Our lives are separate." Weariness slammed into Leanna, pulling her down.

"Did you tell him about Kai?"

"I can't. Just don't feel I can share Kai with him yet."

"Too many feelings to sort out?"

"I have to get used to Bryce's being here first."

Alice gave her a look that said she understood.

Coming home to forget didn't work, Leanna thought as she collected up the sales receipts for the day and cleared the counter of wrapping paper. She'd have to work a little harder.

Chapter 6

Bryce let the jeep idle for a few seconds before shutting off the engine. He propelled himself out of it and looked around. Cars in the Park Service parking lot were packed tighter than sardines, and people came out of the office holding tickets and maps to the island. What did he expect? That he'd have a one-man's island just to be able to get on with the study? The tourist center at Pelican Harbor knew how to generate revenue. And that was the bottom line, money.

A glance at his watch showed it was close to quitting time at the Park Service office and everywhere else. Kip should be hovering in the Piper Cub any minute now. Bryce squinted up at the pale blue sky. And then, the low drone of a plane grew louder as it approached him. Out of the blue, the familiar light aircraft swooped lower in preparation to land.

Good old Kip, and not a moment too soon. Bryce felt the backpack containing the purchases and reassured himself. At least, the trip to the mainland hadn't been a total waste.

Kip made a circle and then landed the plane.

Bryce grinned and waved.

"Ready, boss?"

"Ready." Bryce swung himself in and pulled the door shut.

His Harbor Girl

"Got the films all squared away," Kip said and pulled on the throttle to take off. "The Wildlife Center can't wait to see the pictures. I told them we had some dandies and how you practically hung out of the plane to get them."

"Er...thanks." Bryce strapped himself in and leaned back.

"And how was your day?"

"I got the things I wanted. We have water filters to last till the end of our stay. Just want to make sure we don't fall sick before the work is finished."

As they gained altitude Bryce's thoughts went back to Leanna. What a day it had been! Contrary to his expectations, he hadn't made any headway with her. All he wanted to do was to find out what was on her mind, but instead he'd come away feeling like a rooster chased out of the henhouse. Fine. With his work he had enough on his hands already to try to figure her out. Women!

He glanced at Kip who hummed to himself. Even above the drone of the plane Bryce could hear his tuneless hum, and that was a good sign. That would keep him busy. He noticed little else when flying the plane.

Bryce wasn't the best companion today. Tormented by confusing feelings, he turned his attention to the expanse of blue below. How free it felt to be up here! No worries about past mistakes. He glanced sideways at Kip. He was too engrossed in his prowess as a pilot to be concerned about Bryce's lack of conversation.

"Oh, bury me not on the lone prairie," Kip started belting out after they were airborne for a while.

"Hate to bother you, Kip, but are we almost there yet?" Bryce hoped that would shut him up at least for the time it took to reply.

That annoyed Kip. "Of course not. Do you think this is a bus that you can get off just anywhere?"

"Sorry. I forgot."

But now Kip seemed to have lost his mood for singing. "You see that clearing there? That's where we're headed, so it's close. Hope Fred has dinner waiting for us."

Bryce hoped so too. They should have eaten dinner at one of the restaurants at Pelican Harbor. But Bryce wanted to leave the mainland and forget the heated exchange he'd had with Leanna until he could sort out the workings of his confused mind. An inexplicable feeling of withdrawal came over him, a feeling of defeat and he asked himself how he would he act if he saw Leanna again. Would there be a next time in this crazy situation of theirs?

He huddled in his seat and looked out the window. There, straight ahead, was the clearing.

"Hang on, partner." Kip said used the Western drawl he saved for special occasions. He made concentric circles like an eagle swirling down on carrion. "And we're home."

Kip touched down with two skipping bumps like a child jumping on a pogo stick. "That's because the ground is uneven. Not my fault."

Bryce heaved a sigh of relief. This might be the quick way to get to and from the island, but it kept a man's nerves on edge. Especially if he'd had a quarrel with the woman in his life, or what he had of a life.

He hefted the bag of supplies over his shoulder and jumped off the plane.

Fred came lumbering out. "Back already? I thought you guys would have dinner there. Why didn't you?"

"What? And miss all this? Not a chance." Bryce grinned at him. "What's been going on while we were gone?"

"New wolf tracks."

"Really? Where?"

"Further inland. And I sorted out the radio collaring equipment." Fred led the way into the cabin. "The interview lady wants another interview with you. Come on, what's cooking, huh?" Fred darted Bryce a sly wink.

"Knock it off. What else? Spot any tourists around here?"

"Some."

Bryce shook his head. "That will slow us down."

"Yeah. Well, wash up. Dinner's waiting."

"What are we eating?"

"Spanish rice, beans, venison stew."

Bryce un-shouldered the bag and let it fall on to the table, then stretched out his arms to relax his muscles. Maddening quarrel with Leanna or not, he was bushed and hungry.

The two graduate students stomped in, chattering and thumping each other on the back. Seeing Bryce, they grinned. "We lucked out. Found some moose kills."

One of them set down a green army bag that looked bulky. Bryce knew it contained megaphones and amplifiers for broadcasting wolf howls to locate dens.

"Did you use the trails?" Bryce asked. He lowered himself onto a chair near the heavy table upon which Fred started laying a bowl of stew and another bowl containing tomato-garnished rice.

"Trails and ridges," one of them said. Wearing plaid shirts they looked like rustic lumberjacks, rather than students. Their faces were covered with weeks' growth of beard.

Bryce instinctively passed a hand over his clean-shaven face. No matter how tight the finer amenities of cabin living, he had to shave. No telling when he'd encounter a fastidious wolf pack that might be offended by his personal grooming habits. They wouldn't think much of being studied by a guy looking like a wino on the run from the law.

"The moose remains we found were either calves or very old."

"Figures," Bryce replied with a thoughtful expression. "The healthy moose get away. Hate to say it but the more moose there are, the better the wolves will fare."

"Wolves have dwindled down to a mere fourteen on the island." Fred gulped down Sprite.

"Let's hope that more pups survive each winter, and we find no antibodies when we test them. Because that would mean they're free of parvo virus."

Bryce laid his fork down. As much as he labored over the sorry fate of the wolves, he hated to see moose killed. But the curious law of nature had ordained it that way. Survival of the fittest.

"The remoteness of the island makes it easier to track since there are no hindrances, except for tourists in the summer." Fred got up to put his plate in the sink. A long white apron hung on a hook above the sink as if to offer a challenge to the official dishwasher of the evening.

"Hopefully, they'll taper off at the end of summer. But as long as the ferry service is available they'll keep coming." Bryce's mind slipped back to the time he saw Leanna standing near a clump of bushes. He'd wished he could stop his chest from giving a walloping thump like a triphammer. What the sight of her could still do to him! And with no help from her whatsoever. Of all the crazy, random things, she had to be a tour guide, the very opposite of what he had set out to achieve. Not that he questioned Leanna's choice of work, but it simply got in the way of his professional objectives.

Bryce pushed back his chair and stretched his legs. Sipping coffee, he let the hot liquid simmer in his mouth as he swallowed. God, it felt good and strong, despite the trudges through mud puddles, skin tears on his hand from pulling apart bushes that felt like nettle thorns, and sticky summer heat. At the end of the day it made it all worthwhile to make his notes and take stock of their accomplishments, armed with a cup of steaming hot coffee.

"No, no," Tim said, assuming a mock-serious expression and holding up both hands. "Don't any of you guys get up. We insist. We're doing the dishes. And, please, no applause."

"Thanks, guys. Tomorrow's my turn." Bryce grinned at the two students who affected a dainty walk toward the sink with the plates they had gathered to wash.

"There is a way we could put the presence of tourists to good use." Bryce got up to walk around the cabin. He felt stuffed from eating so much. The penalty for liking Fred's cooking. "Ask them if they heard any wolf howls."

"Uh-huh. That together with aerial tracking would give us the home range of the wolves." Fred got out another stick to whittle.

Bryce suspected that the whittling had the effect of smoking a cigarette on Fred, or chewing gum. It helped him to concentrate or relax as the need arose.

"But, here's one to chew on. Who's going to log the data into the computer? I don't know that stuff and I don't think the students or you have the time once this thing gets going," Fred said.

"You're right." Bryce glanced at the students, hard up to their elbows in sudsy water and washing noisily like toddlers playing in a tub during a bath. "And we can't ask the park employees who man the dock cabin to input data onto our computer. Maybe, I should advertise for someone at the mainland."

Bryce moved to the table crammed with papers, diskettes, books and folders to sift through his file folder. He had made twenty pages of hand notes, besides graphs and tables. But these would have to be logged and stored away. It wouldn't be wise to have them strewn around here. He believed in making backup files to be sent to the Wildlife Ecology Center where Kip made frequent trips. There, his secretary could start printing out hard copies of their work. Documented evidence of their work had to be put into safe hands. He couldn't afford to lose them or have them go out of sequence, which could happen if left in notebooks or sheets of paper.

He pushed the mountain of material on the table away from the edge from which it looked about ready to fall, and looked around, a muscle working in his jaw. Maybe the Park Service officer could post a notice on the mainland. What were the chances that Leanna would apply for the job? Maybe he could engineer it to turn out that way. He'd give it a try. That would get Leanna out of the clutches of that Nolan Packard guy and give her a chance at a better paying job, one that used her intelligence.

Collecting all the loose sheets of paper, he stacked them neatly and let out a sigh of satisfaction. The idea gave new impetus to his work. He could see the stacks of paper dwindling as their contents were entered into the computer.

Bryce gripped the top of the chair and imagined Leanna sitting in it. What could he do to change things between them? To have her love again. Swim clear across the lake, if that would help.

The cabin went suddenly very quiet. The guys had finished washing up and had retreated to their cabin with the insidious-looking bag before they were drafted for other chores. Fred was moving about in the lean-to outside, probably sorting specimens. Kip had taken his camping equipment out to hunker down under the stars. He wouldn't be confined within four walls.

Bryce could finally work without the guys all casting sneaky looks at him, wondering what got his tongue. He sat on the chair with his legs up on the table, crossing them at the ankles, his favorite way of sitting when reading or writing.

He pulled out a note pad and pencil and scribbled in a right-slanted scrawl. "Wanted: A research assistant to log in data, graphs and tables for scientist working on wolf study. Salary negotiable for good worker." The cell phone number stood prominently displayed. If anyone had questions about the job they could call him directly.

Bryce studied the ad and then added a ballpark salary. He grinned as an idea suddenly occurred. It would produce results if Leanna acted in the way he hoped.

He got up and placed the note in a folder, intending to let it settle in his mind before he printed out a copy using fancy bordering on it, the way he'd seen the office secretary do when she had to design invitations for office parties. His secretary would be impressed at the way he created the notice. Satisfied with his work, he printed out several copies of it.

That out of the way, he pulled a bag from under the table and poured out its contents onto the floor. There were masking tapes used as labels for specimens, syringes for injecting wolves with sedatives while radio collaring, and a roll of plastic baggies secured with a rubber band.

The sound of a step broke into the lull of the cabin's living room area. Bryce turned around. Fred walked in the door, his hand still in the gloves used for sorting specimens.

"Need another bag for storing." A bucket holding heavy-duty plastic bags stood in a corner and he pulled one out. Seeing Bryce occupied in his own chore, Fred stopped. "What d'you got there?"

"Making sure we have all the instrumentation we need for radio-collaring." Bryce straightened up and surveyed the items on the floor. "I've made up an ad for a research assistant to help us with the data. I'll be posting it on my next trip to the mainland. Don't know when that's going to be."

Fred's eyes bugged out. He was obviously fascinated by the idea. "Good job. Maybe, we could get that journalist babe to do it." His eyes beamed at the prospect.

"She already works for *The Environmentalist*. I doubt she would be interested."

"Okay. Too bad, though. You lost your chance."

"I'll regret it till the day I die."

Fred made a doleful face and shook out the bag. "Back to cleaning and sorting." He disappeared into the darkening scene outside.

Bryce helped himself to another mug of coffee, went to the open door and stared out. This place looked like the original Garden of Eden in the summer months from what he'd heard and read. He loved being among the trees looking for signs of wolf dens. In the cold winter months in Wisconsin, with the snow lying in thick sheets all around, looking for tracks in the snow had made him feel like he was treasure hunting. Only, they had no treasures to hunt and life had been hard, at least for him.

He leaned against the doorway and let the breeze sift in and flush out the aroma of cooking that still seemed to cling to the inside of the cabin.

The computer workspace grabbed his attention once again. Once the data were entered they would have accomplished their mission. And the only person he saw in his mind's eye, with her fingers dancing over those keys, was Leanna. A slow smile turned up the corners of his mouth. This was a brainwave, if ever there was one. The best he'd ever had.

* * * *

Leanna kept up a steady jog, followed by Kai and Cody. The beach lay calm, lit up by the glow of the sun just dipping into the water like a red plastic pan.

"Hurry up, guys. You're way behind." She stopped for Kai and Cody to catch up then threw herself on the soft white sand. Cody and Kai did the same.

"Is Bryce coming again, Mommy?"

"I don't know." Leanna's heart pumped with an uneasy beat. She hadn't seen him after their terse encounter the last time. Maybe it bode better for them both if he stayed away. The perpetual fear of his finding out about Kai before she was ready to tell him herself clanged in the back of her mind like a racing fire engine.

"Cody likes Bryce too," Kai chanted as they trudged up the hill to the house. "Don't you, Cody?'

To Leanna's annoyance, Cody hung his tongue out and looked at her appealingly. "Be quiet, Kai. You don't know what you're saying." That was all she needed, both of them reminding her how wonderful Bryce was.

Leanna had to sort out feelings of annoyance and anxiety. Annoyance at Bryce and the ever-present worry of Kai being the bone of contention between them, specially now that new plans for The Tug were in the making. A snack bar would attract more customers. Going one step further than just dreaming about it, she'd applied for a small loan at the Citywide Bank.

Half an hour later, the trio crossed the road and walked up the shady avenue of maples.

"Heel, Cody." Leanna waited for him as he came to her side. The run at the beach whipped up an appetite.

"I'm hungry." She smiled at Kai. "Are you?"

Kai nodded.

Leanna laughed. "Let's see. I'll make some spaghetti. Would you like that?"

"Yes," Kai screamed with delight. "Come on, Cody. I'll race you home."

Leanna followed close behind and grinned as Kai and Cody waited for her to open the door. "Want to help me with dinner?" she asked Kai.

Cody gave a soft "woof," as if reminding her that he didn't want to be left out in the important chore of fixing dinner.

"All right. You, too."

She took out a large stainless steel pan, filled it with water and placed it on the burner, which she turned on.

"Want to help me break the spaghetti and put it in when the water starts boiling?"

"Yes."

"I'm going to call Aunty Alice and ask if she'd like to have dinner with us." Leanna hurried into the living room to make her call. She picked up the cordless phone and dialed Alice's number.

"Hello?" Alice's voice came over the receiver.

"Have you eaten? We're making spaghetti. I thought you'd like to come over."

"I'd love to. Give me a minute to wash up. I've been weeding among my azaleas all afternoon."

Leanna smiled as she hung up. Alice and her gardening were like her father and his carpentry. Would be nice if she could get the two of them together. She tried to call her father too. But when she dialed his number, the endless ringing of his phone drummed in her ears. Not there. He must be visiting one of his VFW buddies. It didn't matter; she'd have Alice for company.

Leanna went into the kitchen just in time to see the water boiling. She took out a packet of spaghetti. "Here, open this for me and I'll put it in the pan." Kai put the packet on the kitchen table and, opening it, broke the pasta a little at a time.

"Did I do good, Mommy?"

"You sure did." Leanna dumped the spaghetti into the pan and then took out a small onion to chop and sauté. In a few minutes, the meat sauce and onions simmered in another pan.

The doorknocker on the front door resounded with a thud. "In here, Alice," she called out.

Alice walked in, bearing a round pan covered with an aluminum foil. "Cheesecake." She set it on the table and glanced at Leanna. "How did it go at The Tug?"

"Fair. Summer means tourists. Autumn and winter are another story. But that's all going to change." Leanna stirred the contents of the saucepan, creating a mouth-watering aroma of sautéed onions and lightly seasoned meat sauce. A quick glance assured her the spaghetti bubbled steadily. In a few minutes she could drain the water.

Alice sat at the table, her eyes fixed at Leanna. "Why is that?"

"I've applied for a small loan to add a snack bar to The Tug. If it comes through, I'm planning to make the addition."

Alice did not reply. Leanna's attention riveted on the spaghetti, which she now took over to the sink to drain. It took a few moments for her to realize that Alice hadn't made any comment about her wonderful new idea. She placed the pan on the counter and said, "What do you think?"

"Is it a good idea? What if it doesn't bring in customers?" Alice's eyes widened with concern.

"I've a good feeling about this. In the winter the skiers come to town. If we could serve hot chocolate, bagels and croissants, they would stop to browse and buy. I've seen it done in other places."

Leanna tried not to show the doubt she sometimes felt about this new idea. She had to try it out first. Maybe it would work; she'd never know if she didn't try.

"I hope you're right. Want me to set the table?" Alice got up.

"Yes. The plates are in the top cabinet near the fridge."

Alice stood tiptoe and barely reached the shelf to bring the plates down. She laid them on the table and placed the napkins.

"I know I'm right." Leanna opened the drawer, picked up silverware and placed them near the plates.

Silence fell as they started their meal.

"Heard from Bryce?"

"No." Leanna's mouth drooped slightly.

"And you're not going to say anymore."

"That's right." Leanna twirled the spaghetti on her spoon.

Stuffed with food, Kai started fidgeting in her chair. "Mommy, can I go play?"

"Wash your hands first."

"I've been wanting to have something like The Tug for a long time. Something I can engross myself in." Leanna prodded a string of pasta with her fork, a determined expression on her face.

"To forget Bryce?" Alice said with a deliberate emphasis on the name that made Leanna's heart pop like a balloon.

"Of course not," she replied firmly. But who was she fooling? "I like being in business."

"I wasn't doubting that, but it's a big responsibility."

"I'm over Bryce. That's what you're leading into, isn't it?"

"Just don't want you getting hurt."

"Yes, I know. I won't. I've got too much at stake to live in the past. I want to move on. It's just too bad that Bryce has shown up at such an inconvenient time in my life." Leanna pushed her chair away, picked up her plate and Alice's and stacked it with Kai's in the sink.

"You've got a direction to your life, now. Maybe that's the key." Alice looked convinced of Leanna's determination. She got up. "Here, let me clean up if you have to help Kai with her bath."

"Thanks a ton."

Leanna found Kai on her belly, coloring in her "Scooby Doo" book. "Ready for a bath?"

Kai got up and followed her upstairs.

After half an hour of splashing, Kai was scrubbed and cleaned of sand and dirt, while Cody watched, his face etched in sympathy.

"Out you go." Leanna helped the child into pajamas. "You can watch the "Jelly Bean Show" for a while. And then it's off to bed."

Leanna knew she probably sounded like a drill sergeant. But if she had to bring up Kai, there had better be some rules. She didn't like Bryce breezing in and spreading charm, making her feel like the Wicked Witch of the West in her handling of Kai.

Chores in the kitchen all finished, Leanna walked Alice part of the way to her house. "Want me to work at the store tomorrow?" Alice asked.

"Yes, would you please? I have errands to run." She had to drop Kai off at the daycare and mail supporting documents for her loan application.

* * * *

Leanna picked up her duster to sweep off days' accumulation of dust. Newspapers and magazines Kai had used to cut pictures for her paper dollhouse lay around. A sheet fell from her grasp as she grabbed a swatch of papers. She bent down to pick it up. It had pictures pasted on it breadth-wise. A man, a woman, a little girl and a dog the exact same color as Cody. Great. Now Kai was in search of a father figure. How was she to know the incidents that had shaped Leanna's life? Someday, when Kai was old enough, she would understand. She stared at the picture for a few moments and put it away.

Leanna turned around and took up her dusting again. Immersed in shifting, picking up, mopping and polishing, she failed to hear the sound of the jeep rolling up her driveway.

A knock on the door sent Cody into a barking fit. He went to the door and sat there wagging his tail as if he knew exactly who stood on the other side. Leanna watched in bewilderment.

"Shame on you, Cody. You're supposed to protect me, not grin at every stranger who happens on our doorstep." Leanna kicked away the cloth duster lying at her feet.

She hurried toward the door to see who it was and to send them away so she could get on with the rest of her cleaning. Amazement choked her when she opened the door.

"Bryce!"

For the second time his aura filled the doorway as he stood there, the epitome of languid grace. But this time at her home.

"Alice told me where to find you."

"You don't give up, do you?" Feelings of petulance mixed with confusion overcame her. She remembered his questions the last time there were together.

"Guilty as charged. But this time, we need some help."

He stood at an angle, with an elbow resting against the doorway, thick golden hairs on his forearm glistening like copper wires. His proximity obscured her self-control. No longer completely sure of herself, she determined not to lose her resolve of resisting whatever he came to say.

"We?" She said, feeling his intense gaze meandering over her face. A warm flush stole over her.

"My research associates and I. We need an assistant who will input data, graphs." He straightened and took a thick wad of folded notepaper out of his tee shirt pocket. "I have an ad I would like to post in places you think have high visibility. Since I don't have the time to do it myself I'd appreciate it if you could. Here, would you like to take a look at it?"

Leanna's eyes riveted on the note, and she read the words. They were offering a decent amount of money. What she made now managing the apartments was meager compared to this.

"As you can see, we're not sparing any expense. Our budget is covered by a National Science Foundation grant. We just need the work done"

His voice carried a unique force. The next minute, nonchalance seemed to take over his demeanor. Or so it seemed to Leanna.

She felt a nuzzle against the back of her leg. "Cody!" He peered at Bryce and gave a delighted bark. He shot out from behind her, and, a few seconds later, Bryce and Cody were rolling outside in the grass. Amusement edged with irritation swept through her. They were like children. The only one missing was Kai. There was cleaning to finish and here he was wrestling with Cody. How could she make him leave without seeming rude?

Leanna went into the kitchen with the ads. Opening her recipe drawer, she pulled out a long envelope and stuffed the ads in it. She could post them at the Chamber of Commerce and other public buildings nearby. Back in the living room, she looked out the window to see Bryce get up, brush himself off, and head toward the house with Cody.

Bryce came up the steps taking long strides and entered the living room. Cody trotted behind him with robot minded obedience. Leanna stared at them. How could Cody defect to the enemy camp so easily?

"Now you be a good boy," Bryce said to Cody who seemed to hang on his every word. He turned to Leanna. "Thank you for posting that notice."

"Would you like something cold to drink?" The scene outside sizzled in the late morning sun. She couldn't send her worst enemy back into the heat again without offering a cold refreshment.

Looking surprised, he turned toward her. "Great! I have to meet Kip back at the dock in a hour."

"Kip?"

"He's the pilot of our research plane." Bryce looked around at the room, now partly cleaned and dusted. The large sofa and love seat were attractively covered. Magazines had been put away. The comfortable old room took on a new aspect just by his being there.

"I'll be right back with some lemonade. Or would you prefer a cola?"

"Lemonade."

Leanna returned with the glasses on a tray and handed Bryce his. In doing so, his fingers brushed hers in a moment of electrifying charge.

She moved away with a jerk and placed the tray on the coffee table.

"What's the matter? Afraid I'll seduce you?" His eyebrows quirked in a look of teasing amusement. No one would blame me. Look at you. Even in those jeans and tee shirt, and hair all messed up, you're still tantalizing." An appraising gaze trailed over the length of her body.

They both stood where they were, neither wanting to relax and sit down. Leanna couldn't ease the pounding, like a steel drill, in her chest. "You wouldn't succeed if you tried. You don't know what I'm like anymore."

"I suppose you're right. I thought I knew you." He took a few gulps of his lemonade and put his glass down.

Leanna clung to her glass with a stubborn resolve. He moved toward her, took the glass from her hand and set it on the table. He touched her chin with a finger. "As lovely as always. I have to confess a promise I made to myself."

"A promise?" Her voice came out like a croak. She could kick herself for her gaucheness. His closeness and touch spawned a gamut of perplexing emotions. Screams of frustration stood poised at the back of her throat ready to break out.

Taking an involuntary step back, she created more space between them. "Promise?" She repeated. Her voice failed her when she wanted to sound firm and sure.

"That I would find you again one day, and learn why you left me." His manner had the deliberation of a man who could never be satisfied with a dream. She knew that tone; it meant what he said and it filled her with a crazy assurance.

But that wasn't enough for her. Not now, when year after year, she'd hoped he'd somehow show up. "After all this time, they're only words, Bryce. I won't worry about the promise you made to yourself. I've told you all I have to say about why I did what I did." She felt the tightly strung charge break and found her voice again.

He moved toward her, then seemed to change his mind and appeared resigned to her explanation.

"If you would post the ad, we'd appreciate it. And now, I'm off," he said. "Thanks for this. I mean it. Seems as if we're always saying 'goodbye.'" He gulped down the lemonade in one shot and the next minute he was gone.

Leanna shut the door slowly; unable to believe he'd been here. It felt like the blow-by of a hurricane for which she had to batten down the hatches of the heart for her own protection.

She went into the kitchen drawer, pulled out a copy of the ad and stared at it as an idea thrust itself into her mind. Leanna turned it over and over in her hand absent-mindedly. A few minutes ticked by, and then she made her decision.

Chapter 7

Leanna took a sip of coffee and set the cup down. The sun, slanting through the kitchen window, threw a pool of light on the advertisement beckoning from the table. She picked it up and pondered it. On the plus side, the job duties were interesting and the money very suitable. On the minus side, it meant seeing Bryce every other day. If she got the job, Alice and she could alternate managing The Tug. The ad mentioned that the person was not required to stay on the island.

Leanna could hear Kai calling to Cody in the backyard. If only her own decision could be as simple as a child at play. It would rankle Bryce if she applied for it herself when he'd wanted it posted, especially since she hadn't given him the slightest notion that she might be interested. Her gaze darted to the number at the bottom of the page. Bryce's phone number seemed to burn a hole in the paper. If she called and asked about the position, he'd have the biggest laugh. She couldn't subject herself to that indignity.

Kai came to the window and waved. Leanna waved back. How happy she looked out there, playing with Cody. Leanna opened the patio door that led out of the dining room and walked into the bright, afternoon sunshine.

"Here, Mommy, catch." Kai threw a green rubber ball. Leanna caught it, her fingers feeling Cody's bite marks on it, and laughed at him chasing his tail.

She tossed the ball and off he dashed after it. That would keep him engaged for a few minutes. She sat on the grass and patted the spot next to her. "Come sit by me, Kai. Would you like it if I went to work for Bryce on the island?"

"Can I come too?"

"No, honey. You'll have daycare. But I won't be gone long during the day. You could get a ride home with Cecily's mom."

"Can I have Cecily come over and play?"

"Yes, if Alice or I am home with you."

"Can Bryce come and play with us?"

"I…I don't know." Leanna nibbled on a blade of grass. Between earning extra money and the pointed aversion to working so closely with Bryce, her sensibilities were being pulled every which way. Leanna's hand quivered and she threw away the sliver of grass.

Her temples throbbed with the excitement of a daring decision about to be taken. She didn't know if she'd be able to pull off working with Bryce and keep her composure, smell the familiar cologne that he carelessly splashed on his face—something she'd seen him do so many times. Or watch the way his eyes squinted when the sunlight hit them. If only she didn't need the job!

Leanna took a deep breath and questioned her sanity; she didn't know how this would affect her. She prided herself on thinking she didn't need him in any way, and now, she discovered that the job would provide quite a tidy sum. She was doing it to expand the store.

She would apply for the job. She was stronger now, not the infatuated student she once was. She could handle it.

Leanna got up. "I have to go inside and do some work."

"Can I stay out and play some more?" Kai rolled over and sat up, her hair tousled.

"Sure."

Leanna went into the kitchen and looked at the crisp white piece of paper lying against the varnished wood of the table. Then she picked up the cordless phone on the sideboard in the dining room, and dialed the number. The seconds that passed with each ring cut off her resolve. Why not hang up now, forget the whole thing and just continue managing the apartments? The ringing stopped.

"Hello?" Bryce's deep languorous voice could still send quivers through her.

"Hello, Bryce. This is Leanna." She anticipated Bryce tensing up after she'd played so hard to get. "I'd like to apply for the job you asked me to post."

A few interminable seconds of silence followed. "Okay by me. Just file your application with the Park Service office. They're collecting all the applications for us."

"Just thought I'd let you know. If you didn't want me to apply for any reason, I'd understand." Leanna tried to sound detached.

"I've no objections. Wouldn't be right for me to object," Bryce said.

A coldness seemed to drift through the line, like a blast of arctic air zapping a sultry oasis. She sensed indifference. But if this was going to be uphill all the way, she might as well try for the job. Obviously, he didn't want her to apply, but politeness prevented him from objecting.

"I'm glad you don't mind," Leanna said with forced lightness. "If you change your mind just let me know."

"I will."

His words cut like diamond on glass. And she'd opted to work for this man!

Leanna set the phone down slowly, feeling like a drowning rat trying to keep afloat. She had never allowed self-pity to encroach in all the difficult moments of life. But now, it reared its insistent head, when all she wanted was to raise Kai and give her a reasonably comfortable life.

* * * *

Leanna changed into khaki pants and shirt and glanced quickly at the clock. Kai had to be dropped off at the daycare. She also wanted to see Alice at The Tug before going to the Park Service landing site to fly to the island on the research plane. She went to the hall closet to pick up the backpack. What would Bryce do now that she'd gotten the job? Would he sulk? Act cocky?

"Ready?" Leanna walked with Kai to the door, car keys clenched in her hand.

"Can I go on the plane too sometime, Mommy?"

"Maybe." She couldn't deny Kai her slightest wish. But to expect Bryce to give in to that was something else.

Leanna drove the station wagon, which was now repaired and almost good as new, past the slowly awakening harbor town. A week ago, she'd told Nolan she'd applied for this job, and that she'd have to resign if she got the offer. He'd seemed surprised, and then accepted the idea. "If you must, you must," he'd said.

At the daycare, she helped Kai out of the car. "I don't know when I'll be home today because it's the first day at my new job. So Alice will bring you home. Is that okay, sweetie?"

Kai nodded. Leanna gave her a hug and led her to the entrance.

Satisfied that Kai would be all right, Leanna got into her car and drove to The Tug.

Alice was all excited. "There's no telling what might develop."

"You wish." Leanna tried to look stern. But she couldn't stop the unreasonable thumping of her heart, and she wondered if she *did* want anything to develop with Bryce again.

"Don't worry about Kai. I'll bring her home and keep her company."

Leanna gave her a hug. "Got to go."

She hurried out of The Tug, the gravel crunching under the tread of her well-worn walking shoes. The sensible khakis she wore were adequate for the task ahead, even the prospect of seeing Bryce. She got into her station wagon and drove to the Park Service office. This was strictly professional, no need to get uptight. It was all about money and the means of earning some.

The research plane stood waiting, just as he had mentioned on the phone when he'd called to give her instructions on getting to the island. A man, probably the pilot, was examining the wing struts, and straightened up when he saw Leanna.

"Leanna Reed? I'm Kip. I'll be taking you over to the island." He came forward and shook her hand. "Hop in."

He helped her in and then settled into his seat.

"All set? Hold on tight. Can't understand why Bryce gets so nervous in this bird," Kip said as he taxied and lifted off.

Leanna didn't know whether to laugh or let out a shriek of horror. Was this the only way to go to work every other morning? She tried to focus on the bright blue yonder.

"Not bad, huh? The view from up here, I mean." Kip jerked his head in her direction.

"No…"

"Relax. You'll get used to it. Takes only twenty minutes. I'll set her down easy."

Kip was as good as his word. Half an hour later, something that seemed an eternity to her, he brought the plane down with a soft landing. From where she sat Leanna saw Bryce come out of the cabin and watch them alight. She felt the intense charge of Bryce's gaze fixed on her as she stepped lightly off the plane with Kip helping her down.

"How was the flight?" Bryce's features softened into a half-smile. "Kip is the final word on flying this aircraft. He's been doing this a long time."

"So I see." Leanna smiled at Kip.

"Don't let her fool you. She's as jumpy as you are on the plane. Can't think why you're all so nervous." Kip threw up his hands and disappeared in the direction of the storage shed, lugging a thick coil of rope.

"Watch your step." Bryce guided her with a hand lightly at her elbow as they went up a set of wooden steps. The pressure of his touch was protective and she was grateful for that.

"Not tipsy from the ride, are you?" Bryce chuckled as he pushed the cabin door open.

"No." That wasn't quite true, but she didn't want to sound like a sissy, unable to bear the slight discomfort of a ride on a light plane.

"Step into my office. And excuse the mess. I really need the graphs and tables put into the computer."

Leanna looked around the front room of the cabin, enlivened with curiosity. So this was where he hid out.

"Interesting place you have here," Leanna said. Her gaze swept over the piles of books and papers shoved to the far corner of the heavy wooden table on which also stood the computer. Little smiley faces danced merrily all over the screen.

It all left her a little breathless. She was reminded of the time they were together in college. This was a mistake, thinking she could hack it here, with him being so close. How would she get through the days and weeks ahead, and concentrate on the job to be done? For a moment, she felt awkward. She took a deep, cleansing breath. She'd do her best.

"You've been hard at work, I see," Leanna said, trying not to let his handsome physical presence unsettle her. But standing here with his books and papers brought back memories, which she had tried to push away.

Bryce dragged a couple of chairs close to the computer.

"Now." He pulled out some hand-written notes and stacked them together. "I need this wolf-monitoring information put into the computer or I'll lose it in all this shuffle. Later on, we'll need to put in the radio collaring data as well."

He saw her look at the dining table that held his large duffel bag. "In there we have our equipment, syringes and tranquilizer. We weigh, ear tag and measure them and examine them for parasites. Then we let them go."

Leanna blew out a breath. "That's a relief. When you said 'radio collaring' I had an impression of the poor things being harassed."

"Not really. That's the whole point of the research. To see how we can better their environment."

Leanna glanced through the notes made in Bryce's familiar slanting handwriting. "Where did you get all this information?"

"From howling surveys, wolf observations of the public, winter tracking surveys."

"You track wolf in the winter?"

"We will be. But not here. The data we have now are from earlier studies." Bryce leaned back in his chair. "How was the ride getting here?"

His expression grew serious and his back became ramrod straight as he watched her with a keenly observant eye.

She tried not to meet his gaze. Those eyes still had the power to mesmerize her and they melted her willpower into a haze of forgotten resolutions. She'd have to do better than this, such as devising a means of immunizing herself to his disarming ways. Right. Maybe a touch of voodoo.

"You mean coming over by light plane? I'm still trying to figure out if I liked it or not."

Bryce chuckled. "I understand. But there's no way of getting here in a timely manner. Unless you choose to stay here in our cabin." His mouth turned upward into a wicked grin causing a slow flush to suffuse her face.

Her chin lifted up. "That wasn't exactly what I had in mind." A sting shot through her reply.

"Okay, okay. Just a thought." His voice bubbled with amusement, much to her chagrin. She probably sounded like a prima donna insisting she be given special privileges. But she couldn't worry about her image. Look where her passion had gotten her the last time!

"Just one thing." Leanna had been bugged with the question ever since Bryce had called and offered her the job. It took him a long time to call with the offer. "Were there many other applicants for this job?" Her voice held an inflection that gave away her curiosity.

Bryce's face softened into an amused smile. "What's bothering you? Don't tell me you think I hired you so I could lure you here to seduce you. Now, what would that do to me as an equal opportunity employer?"

Leanna flushed. Her question wasn't meant to sound so transparent. "I'd just like to know, that's all. Surely, it's a legitimate question." She floundered before the brilliance of his look.

"You can set your suspicious little mind at rest. I had to wade through a stack of applications. But you were the most qualified. You should know that with your college education."

"Yes, but I didn't finish graduate school." This fact had always hung above her head like a sword. It was something she'd always regret.

"You have the courses required to work with the graphs we need put into the computer." A brisk, business-like tone entered his voice, alerting her to the work she had to do.

Leanna paged through the stack of papers and file folders. "I think I can handle this."

"A few hours every time you're here will get the work done. I'm going outside to see if Kip needs any help hauling stuff to the shed."

Bryce pushed the chair back and got up, his hand resting lightly on the back of Leanna's chair. She felt his hand's presence, especially when it seemed to linger near the nape of her neck for a moment longer than necessary.

She shifted uneasily in the chair and tried to conquer her involuntary reactions to him.

The next moment Bryce strode out the door. The studied deliberation of his movements made Leanna wonder if he was suppressing something he had to say. She couldn't forget their last encounter. It had been bitter and full of suspicions on his part and resentment on hers. Now, it appeared as if he had called a truce in order to get his work done.

She dragged her attention back to the computer screen and scrolled down to read the filenames. Then she opened a few files to see what they contained. No problem. In the days to come she'd become as familiar with them as her own backyard.

Relaxing as she heard Bryce pick up his duffel bag and haul it outside, she turned to the pages of figures, jottings, and graphs in front of her. With thoughtful deliberation, she began the task of putting them in the computer.

Leanna didn't have to look at the keys. Speed and accuracy were the hallmarks of her keyboarding. After a few minutes of concentration, the work progressed rapidly and she breathed easier. This wasn't so bad. The graphs made sense. They had to do with wolf and moose census so that a correlation could be found between wolf population and the numbers of moose at any given time.

Outside, she heard Bryce and Kip talking and their heavy footfalls echoed as they trudged to and from the storage shed. The Piper Cub aircraft stood in the clearing not far from the cabin. Kip guffawed. Leanna turned her mind to the graphs. With Bryce out of the way she could get on with her work.

* * * *

Bryce felt the drag of the wind as he swung his duffel bag into the plane, while Kip checked the aircraft.

"How are we doing on fuel?" Bryce leaned against the side of the plane and watched him. He still couldn't get over the fact that Kip had done numerous aerial tracks with other researchers. He knew this contraption like the topography of his own palm, and nothing about flying fazed him.

"We're okay for today, especially since the Cessna 80 will be bringing aviation fuel from Wisconsin sometime today." Kip went around the rear of the plane. "They *are* dropping it off today, aren't they?"

"As far as I know." Bryce had spoken to Aero Service Aviation, the company they had leased the plane from a few days ago. It was their responsibility to supply fuel at regular intervals. And so far, they had delivered.

"Good. Because, if they don't, we'll be hurting for fuel."

Bryce let out a short breath and looked up at the sky. "It's clear for taking a moose census, although there's a rising wind."

"Not a problem. How long you figuring we'll take up there?"

"An hour. A couple of hours, maybe. I'd better tell Leanna."

Bryce walked into the cabin in slow, measured steps and stood by the door watching her work, her back toward him. The bent of her head, hair coiled in a thick knot revealed the delicate nape of her neck, which peeped out of the boyish shirt collar.

Bryce tried to avert his eyes and concentrate on what he'd come to say while Kip waited outside, raring to take off in his bird.

He cleared his throat. "Leanna."

She turned around to face him, surprise showing on her face. "Yes?"

"Kip and I are taking off on an aerial survey. We'll be gone for an hour or two, tops. Carry on with your work and help yourself to anything from the cooler." He pointed to the small box-like container that likely held only very necessary items like soft drinks.

Formality invaded his tone. It wouldn't do if she had the slightest inkling that the sight of her sitting there in this strictly bachelor environment unsettled him. "How's the data entry going?"

"Very well. It's actually making sense." Her forehead had been etched with small lines of concentration. But now, as she spoke to him, her eyes were wide and lustrous. He'd make a fool of himself if cornered by those eyes for too long, and he hadn't forgotten how angry they could look, and pained. If he had a penny for every time she used her eyes as a weapon to hurt him, he'd be a very rich man.

"Good," Bryce said. The situation they found themselves in smacked of artificiality at best. The last time they had been together she'd looked like she'd have liked to bop him one. What chance had he that she'd be well-inclined toward him now? "See you later."

Bryce strode out of the cabin, aware that Leanna still watched him. What did a woman like that think about? He thought he knew. Turned out he was dead wrong. Well, getting up into the wide blue yonder in a light plane looking for moose should help forget woman problems.

"Let's go, Kip," he called out to Kip who looked bored.

"Thought you'd never come out." He had a wicked grin.

"Yeah, yeah. Up and at it." Bryce hauled himself into the Piper Cub and took the seat next to the pilot's.

Kip got in and strapped himself in and Bryce did the same.

"Now," Kip said, putting on his special aviator's glasses, "what are we looking at?" He started taxiing out in the limited airstrip that had been cleared of all the trees and lifted off.

"Wolf herds...dens. Can you buzz us to a hundred feet so we can get a good look?" Bryce didn't want Kip to get any closer although he angled for any opportunity to "buzz" closer.

"I can get down to seventy-five feet. Sure you don't want me to?"

"No, because we don't want to scare them away either. They feed on birch, aspen and balsam fir. So be especially cautious when you encounter those kinds of trees." Bryce took out a pair of high-powered binoculars and studied the scene as they ascended rapidly. He detected movement below. Hefty bull moose. "You can start buzzing at a hundred feet."

Kip needed no further encouragement. Bryce could see that this gave his pilot a chance to practice his aerobatics. "No fancy stunts," Bryce said. Then he held his breath.

* * * *

Leanna got up and stretched. Bleary-eyed from staring at the computer screen for so long, she tried to focus on her watch to see the time. Well past two o' clock. It had been almost three hours since she'd started work on the notes Bryce had left for her.

She opened the cabin door and squinted into the bright glare. Bryce and Kip should be back from their aerial tracking anytime now. Then it would be time to go home. Three hours on the days that she came over to the island was enough time to input Bryce's data. This way, the rest of the day could be spent with Kai. Today, Leanna couldn't wait to see her and listen to tales about Cody.

A low drone drifted toward her and she looked skyward. Up above the maples the Piper Cub hovered in preparation for landing. It made a horrendous sound and finally landed in the clearing near the cabin.

Bryce got out first. He saw Leanna and waved. "How're you getting along with the work?"

"I'm done for today." The figures and graphs had given her a headache, and seeing him there, tall and handsome did little to relieve it.

As he walked into the cabin, Bryce seemed to fill the entire rustic interior of it, with wind-blown hair and the cotton shirt open at the collar to reveal a bronzed, sinewy neck.

Leanna moved toward the cooler and took out a can of cola, her fingers tightening around it. She opened it with a pop and took a sip and savored it, feeling its soothing coolness slowly dribble down her parched throat. The ice-cold liquid eased her, anesthetizing her from Bryce, who walked toward the table and offloaded his heavy duffel bag.

"Was there a drop off of aviation fluid?" Bryce asked, small lines rippling across his broad forehead.

"No. Should there have been one?" An odd question, she thought, when she'd been busy staring at a stack of notes and a computer screen.

"No drop off of fuel, Kip." He shook his head slowly at Kip, who had just walked in.

"Then we're stuck. We have nothing until they drop it off."

"They were scheduled to fly over today with it. Wonder what could have happened?" Bryce dug into his duffel bag and pulled out his cell phone. "No sense in waiting. I'm going to call them."

Leanna watched and waited with a feeling of dread as he pressed the numbers and spoke into the phone. So what did this mean? That there would not be enough fuel to go home? Surely they could at least fly her back.

She thought of Kai waiting for her, probably worried. And the alternative if she were truly stuck here. Under the same roof with Bryce. Oh, no. She wouldn't have any of that!

Conversation over, he clapped the phone shut. He tilted his brow and glanced at her uncertainly. "Looks like you'll have to camp here for the night."

"What?" Her voice rang with exasperation. Her worst fears were coming true. "You can't be serious. I have a child to get back to."

Leanna knew her voice had a harshness she didn't care to display at this point. Bryce was her employer; it behooved her to control her natural annoyance, but she had just slipped into a predicament she wanted to avoid desperately.

"I know. We'd have tried our level best to get you home if we had the fuel. But there is none. So, as I said before, you'll have to overnight it here." His brows knit together in a thoughtful expression. "Look, I don't want to detain you here any more than you want to stay, but there is no other way. You weren't exactly thinking of swimming across the lake, were you?"

Despite her rising aggravation, she couldn't help seeing the humor at the thought of her swimming across. Yes, she'd do that, if she thought it would get her away from him.

She composed herself and ignored his little joke.

"When are you getting the fuel in?" If the drop-off source failed to show up the next day, most likely she would be camping here for a while.

"Tomorrow. They've promised us that. They have some problems with the Cessna that they use for their delivery. And they don't have another plane to spare."

She crushed the empty coke can and felt the aluminum bend under the pressure of her grasp. A feeling of disappointment mixed with apprehension washed over her. There wasn't a thing she could do until they refueled the plane.

"So, I really have no choice," she said slowly, her voice ebbing away as she wondered about Kai. She'd have to call and let them all know.

"No. And the sooner you come to terms with it the better." A slight edge seeped into his tone and a muscle twitched in his jaw.

The encroaching heat of the day, tiredness and disappointment suddenly burst upon her like a dam with its floodgates open. A surge of annoyance welled up in her. What did he think? That she was the ultimate brat?

"What do you take me for? A spoiled child?" The words came out in a tumble. There they stood, the two of them, like children quarreling over the rules of a game.

The next minute, Leanna drew in a deep breath. Maybe she had behaved unreasonably. Still, she didn't have to concede the fact. After all, he had the responsibility to get her back to the mainland after today's work session.

"So hard to overlook it, especially when you behave like one." He moved his shoulders in a shrug of anger. The next moment, he came close, watching her intensely.

"Whether you like it or not you'll have to spend at least tonight here, depending on the availability of the fuel tomorrow. You have two choices. You can mope about the rest of the time, or make the best of the situation we're in. Don't worry, I don't want you staying here any more than you do." His voice dripped acid.

Leanna took an abrupt step back as her mind worked furiously. It wouldn't do to appear peevish especially since she had to depend on him to get home. Then there was the job. She took a quick breath. "My thoughts exactly," she said, anger welling up. Did he empathize at all that she had a child at home? "Just that I'm concerned about Kai. She's going to be worried." And that was the truth.

From the corner of her eye she saw Kip leave the cabin.

"Leanna," Bryce said, drawing closer, his voice low with feeling. "I understand you're concerned about your daughter." His hands reached her shoulders and he pulled her to him. "If you could see yourself…" His mouth closed over hers in a moment blending feeling and fury, for the longest time, it seemed. Until she struggled and broke loose.

"No, I don't think you do," Leanna said." It's work all the way and people don't matter, even if it's a small child."

His Harbor Girl

Bryce moved away, his body appearing slack. "If that's what you think, fine. Now," he said, handing her the cell phone, "call and tell them you can't get across today." Then he strode out the cabin door.

Leanna glanced at her watch. The dial showed a quarter to four. Where had the time gone? Alice would still be at The Tug.

She dialed the number and waited as it rang.

"Hello?" Alice's high-pitched voice flowed through the phone line

A wave of relief rippled through Leanna. How good it felt to talk to Alice. She'd missed them and she'd been away only for the day. And now, she couldn't get home.

"Alice, it's me."

"How are you, dear? How is your new job?" Alice clearly seemed to be in a mood to talk. Leanna would have to get to the point quickly.

"I like it fine. Listen, Bryce won't be able to have the plane bring me home today. The fuel has to come in from Wisconsin and they are having difficulties with the shuttle that's supposed to have dropped it off." Leanna took a breath before she told her the rest of it. Alice was going to love this.

"Which means you'll have to stay the night there?"

"Yes, I'm afraid so."

"Don't apologize. Maybe things are going to work in your favor and Bryce's."

Leanna felt a stab of impatience. Alice was a dear, but she still lived in the previous century. She wanted desperately for "things to work out" between her and Bryce, just for Kai's sake, even though too much had happened in both their lives.

"No, no, you don't understand. I don't want to stay here, but I'm going to have to until they bring me back tomorrow."

She tried to suppress the sharpness in her voice. "Is Kai with you? Could you put her on the phone?"

A few seconds later Leanna heard Kai's childish lilt, something that never failed to delight her. "Hi, baby. I'll have to stay on the island today."

A short pause followed. "Aren't you coming home, Mommy?" The disappointment in her daughter's tone clenched at her heart. Steeling herself, she said, "No, sweetie. The plane's out of fuel. I'll be there as soon as I can tomorrow." *I hope,* she whispered under her breath.

Leanna handed the phone back to Bryce who entered the cabin bringing in a bundle of sheets and a sleeping bag. He looked at her. Was it her imagination or did she detect a shade of concern flit across those granite features?

"I called home and told them I'd be home tomorrow, if you'll be able to fly me over."

"All we need is the fuel. Soon as that gets here you get to go home." He busied himself with finding a place to stack the bundle in the already crowded cabin.

"Naturally, we'll have to find a place for you to sleep in. You can use my room. It's cramped, not the luxury you're probably used to, but it's clean and I've been comfortable there."

Of course! The minor details of where she would spend the night! She was even more anxious to escape him. "That's fine." She kept her voice even as she looked away.

"Now, if you'll excuse me, I have dinner to see to." He moved to the kitchen area and wrapped an apron around his chest.

Despite the tension intensity of the sudden kiss, which was more like a tidal wave than a gentle breeze, Leanna felt a chuckle coming on. He looked funny with the apron tied

His Harbor Girl

around his middle, like an overgrown kid posing as a short order cook.

Trying to sound nonchalant, she said, "Would you like me to help?" She'd rather have kept away from him for the rest of the evening.

"If you like. We're having leftover venison stew. You could make the salad. There are some tomatoes and cucumbers in the crisper." He nodded toward the refrigerator.

The "crisper" consisted of a small corner in the refrigerator. Here, Leanna found a plastic bag containing plump, juicy tomatoes and fresh-looking cucumbers. She washed these and chopped them up and put them in a large plastic dish. "How many are there for dinner?"

"Just you, me, and Kip. The others have gone to our Wisconsin research lab for a few days' work."

An hour later, they sat around the table finishing the meal which, to Leanna's surprise, tasted exceptionally good, even though she could hardly eat. She and Bryce sat there like bookends sharply aware of each other.

"Who cooked the venison?" she asked Bryce when they were finished eating.

"I did." Bryce sounded as cool as if he were announcing the weather.

Leanna's eyes widened with surprise. "When did you turn into a good cook?"

"Since I've been 'batching' it, living out of cans got old."

"You surprise me." She tried hard to keep the wonder out of her voice.

"There's a lot you don't about me, Leanna. As I'm sure you realize"

His voice, soft and sensuous, caressed the air she breathed. Or so it seemed. She had to get out of this cabin as soon as she could. Too bad she couldn't fly across the lake like the seagulls she and Kai often watched.

Chapter 8

Leanna pushed the window open wider so the cool air could ease into the room. A small nightlight glowed in the corner and she glanced at the alarm clock, which showed midnight. She was unable to sleep; her worried mind kept flitting back to Kai and she wondered what was happening at home. She'd never been away from her overnight before. Perhaps, the time had come to let Kai fend for herself a little. No harm in that.

Silence cloaked the cabin with only the occasional hoot of an owl. She wondered if Bryce was coiled up in the sleeping bag he'd lugged in from the storage shed.

She opened the door and peeked into the living room area. Dark shapes of furniture emerged in the film of moonlight streaming in from an open window. But the floor showed bare where a sleeping figure should have been. Where was Bryce? More to the point, why was she looking for him? Curiosity, Leanna thought fiercely. She merely wanted to know what the host of these rustic living quarters was up to.

A locked door barred the entrance to the other room, so he couldn't be in there. The cabin felt stuffy. What if a bear were to appear if she opened the door? She'd take a chance. The acrid atmosphere in the cabin made her claustrophobic, and she needed fresh air.

She pushed open the front door with a palpitating heart and took a sniff of the cool, refreshing air.

A little way toward the storage shed a small fire glowed next to a tent. It looked as if Bryce and Kip were camping out.

Hugging Bryce's borrowed robe around her, Leanna stepped out onto the muddy pathway wearing sneakers.

A gruff voice floated over. It was Bryce. "What are you doing outside?" His voice had none of the deep, velvet quality it usually held. In the silence of the woods, it took on a harsh, flat tone, annoyed almost.

"I couldn't sleep," Leanna said in a matter of fact voice. She really didn't owe any explanations. "And it felt hot and stuffy in my room."

"Sorry we don't have air conditioning, but we have to rough it for the kind of work we do."

"You really don't like me, do you?" Leanna blurted out. Having had enough of his sarcasm, she knew there wasn't going to be any tactful repartee with this man in the middle of the night, in the middle of nowhere.

"I wonder why." Bryce's features looked stern in the dancing flames of the small wood fire.

Leanna shivered. Out here, the brisk air invaded a person like a chilled blanket. But she preferred this to the choking atmosphere in the cabin.

The contours of his body encased in jeans and a sweatshirt showed in the flickering light. His hair, brushed back, looked thick. Somehow, even in the faint, opaque light, Bryce had a fresh glow, as if he'd just showered, and the tantalizing scent of spicy cologne skimmed her nostrils, stirring in her a heady feeling of desire. *Whoa, this won't do.*

She came closer and stood a few steps away from where he sat on a log, poking at the fire with a long stick.

"I've given up trying to figure you out. And, in answer to your question, no, I don't dislike you." Bryce stared at the flames, a handsome profile etched against the darkness.

He turned sideways, glanced at Leanna, and took in the robe she was wearing.

She tried to ignore the pointed glance, now tinged with curiosity. The intensity of his look sent a tremor through her.

"You can sit down. I won't bite," he said.

"I prefer to stand." The cabin would have been more tolerable than this, stuffy or not. Returning to it seemed the sensible thing to do. Yet, she wanted to stay and prove to herself that Bryce's attractiveness, grouchy mood and all, was no match for her strong resolve to resist it.

Another voice, a snide one this time, screeched in her brain, asking if that was *really* what she was thinking. Like the bravado of a child whistling in the dark.

Leanna shifted to the other foot, and decided to stay outside indefinitely.

"Afraid of me, are you? Don't worry, I won't get my evil hands on you." A devilish grin spread across his face.

"I wasn't even considering that." Leanna's chin rose with a new found resolution. His male ego had been dented. Something in the incline of his head indicated it, despite the roughness of his voice; the wall of pride seemed to be eroding.

"Where's Kip?" She felt her body slacken with the knowledge of having won this little skirmish of words.

Bryce got up and put out the fire with a few sprinkles of the water he had near him in a small bucket.

"He's out camping near the Ridge, a few miles from here. I would have gone too if I didn't think you might be afraid to stay alone."

"Why would I be afraid?"

Bryce shrugged. "Alone, at night, in a cabin in the woods." He took a step forward. "I see now that I'm wrong."

There was a drawl in the voice and his gaze enveloped the robe that fell loosely around Leanna, burying her in its vastness.

Minty breath assailed her. Like musk extracted from the sperm whale, it was heady. Leanna moved back instinctively. He gave a soft, hollow laugh. "What are you afraid of? Yourself? That's it, isn't?"

"Don't flatter yourself that I can't resist you," she said calmly.

Bryce's hand went to her chin and lifted it gently. "Let's find out, shall we?"

Moving closer, he enveloped her body under the robe. Hands wandered the length of her, intensity and passion in his fingers. He'd probably guessed she had nothing on but bra and panties. His invitation was a bristling challenge, hard to resist, and it opened up the floodgates of her own desire. She felt like a breathless girl of eighteen. Her feelings had nothing to do with the self-control that had kept her going all these years.

Leanna wanted the moment to go on and yet, she knew the timing was wrong. Although aching for the fulfillment of his lovemaking, she pulled away in exasperation and her pulse skittered alarmingly. Back to square one!

"Conscience bothering you?" His words dripped with sarcasm. "Up to your games again I see." A muscle worked in his jaw and his hands dropped.

Leanna stared. "I never played any games, Bryce. I never really existed for you, remember?"

Even with the hurt welling up inside, Leanna sensed that all Bryce must have seen was a fickle woman who had a sudden change of mind. But he had been in a work-ridden haze all those years ago and she wasn't about to tell him that they were going to have a baby and the right thing to do was to marry her.

She remembered coming to the realization of what was happening, when she'd missed a period, and then another. Forcing herself not to think about it while nursing her mother had helped. But the morning sickness had started with a vengeance. Look at what could happen when passion ran unchecked!

Leanna shook herself free of the memories that still held her fast. She turned away from the glow of the fire; the familiar bongo drum beat pounding inside her chest. She knew what it meant. Bryce still had the power to cause havoc, but this time, Leanna had her own plans.

"I always knew you were there. I wasn't that buried in my work."

"It's obvious, isn't it?" Leanna insisted on making him see what she'd realized.

"What?"

"That you and I can't make it together as a couple. Only as employer and employee. Let's leave it at that."

"If that's what you want." Hurt showed through in his voice, the hurt of a man who felt abandoned. Or was it wounded pride again?

Leanna turned around to run back into the cabin. But her foot caught in a mesh of surface roots of a tree, causing it to twist. As she fell, her palms grazed the stony ground.

"Oh!" She cried out in pain.

Bryce strode hurriedly toward the crumpling form. He knelt down and touched her face with gentle fingers. "Are you all right? Here, let me help you up."

Leanna attempted to raise herself slowly. "I can't." She fell back on her elbows, her foot throbbing.

"You'd better lie still." Bryce slipped his left hand deftly around her and lifted her. "Hold on to me. Looks like I'll have to carry you inside."

Leanna sat up, dazed by the fall. Trying to apply weight on her foot only hurt it even more. "Something's wrong."

"You may have sprained it. Hang on."

Despite her reluctance, she held on as he lifted her and walked toward the cabin.

He cradled her in his arms, walked up the steps and kicked the front door open. Darkness enveloped them. He swung around slowly and switched on the light, then laid her on the floppy couch. "Let's take off your shoe and look at it."

His hands felt cold as he removed the sneaker and examined her foot. "There's a slight swelling. Better put some ice on it."

He pulled out a large men's handkerchief from his jacket on the hook by the door, and filled it with ice cubes from the icebox. He sat on the couch and placed the ice pack on her foot. "That feel better?"

"The swelling should go down by tomorrow." He raised her head and plumped a cushion under it. "Comfortable?"

Leanna nodded. "Thanks." She found herself staring up into those eyes of his, losing herself as if in an endless pool, drawn and mesmerized by their depth. Her palms felt the corded strength of his muscles as his arms encircled her, and she knew she wouldn't be able to resist him. But she wasn't about to make a fool of herself either.

He was gazing at her too. Their eyes locked and it seemed an eternity passed while each refused to make a move, as if holding onto the moment. Bryce traced the lines of her face and lowered his head.

"And now, my payment." He bent down and kissed her on the mouth. His mouth was soft, yet demanding, leaving her breathless. She found herself encircling his neck with her arms and returning his long kiss. All of her loneliness and confusion melded together in one upsurge of devouring yearning and she clung to him.

"You little tantalizer," he murmured.

The next second, he pulled away. "If you prefer, I'll put you in my bed." He inclined his head toward the bedroom she'd occupied. "Without me in it, of course," he added in a hurry, getting off the couch and sitting back on his haunches.

"I'd like that," she replied in a dull voice, knowing well what she felt was disappointment. Where had all her resolve gone? She seemed frozen in a state of limbo where decisions and actions were a mockery.

At last, she fought to control her swirling emotions. He had no business taking advantage of her weakened condition. "No business at all," she muttered, not realizing that she had said the words out loud.

"Pardon?" He surveyed her from the side of the couch. "Did you say something?"

Leanna shook her head. "Just talking to myself. What happened between us shouldn't have."

"Why do you say that?"

"Because neither of us meant it, and you know it." The edge in her voice cut through the silence in the cabin.

"You read minds too?" His voice reeked with sarcasm.

Bryce stood up. "I'd like to turn in for the night. If you still want to use my room, I'll take you there."

He could have been the weatherman announcing the advent of a cold front, judging from his sudden detachment. That suited her just fine. So why did her heart ache? She'd give anything to feel the indifference that Bryce obviously did.

Leanna nodded, not trusting herself to speak.

He scooped her up as easily as a child would pick up a toy, pushed the bedroom door open with his foot, and deposited her on the bed. "There. Now, try and get some sleep." He moved toward the door.

The thin aura of the nightlight threw his features into detailed relief, making them appear like those of a statue. Obviously, he wasn't going to give her an inkling of what he was thinking.

"Do you want an aspirin?"

"I think I'd better have one." The throbbing would probably continue all night.

He went into the kitchen and brought back a couple of aspirin, and handed them to her with a glass of water.

She swallowed them and handed back the glass. "Thanks."

"Goodnight." He stepped out of the room and pulled the door shut behind him.

Leanna yanked the light sheet over herself and glanced at the clock. Two o'clock. Her ankle ached. How long would she be detained in this outlandish cabin?

She turned her head on the pillow and let out a sigh. She had no wish to share the cabin with Bryce. She lay there, mesmerized by the faint glow of the nightlight. The first thing tomorrow, she'd see about getting home.

* * * *

Back at her house, Leanna went out into the patio with the day's mail after lunch, and savored the delight of being home these past few days. She laid the mail on the table and, sitting on one of the chairs, raised her foot to examine her ankle. The swelling had subsided, and so had the pain.

A breeze shimmied off the lake, lifting her hair, and she squinted her gaze down the hill to the lake. A few boaters sailed idly. She glanced at a stack of mail on the white wicker patio table and plucked a long, white envelope from the pile.

She was almost afraid to open it in case they'd refused her the loan. She held the envelope as if it were a rattler she was holding by the tail. Then she got a hold of herself, slit open the envelope and shook out the letter. The letterhead of the Citywide Bank grabbed her attention.

"Dear Ms. Reed," it said, "We are pleased to offer you the loan in the amount of..." It stated the amount requested and advised her to call for an appointment.

Leanna breathed a sigh of relief. She could now go ahead with her plans. She laid the letter on the table and placed a copper paperweight on it. Her dream of adding a snack bar to The Tug would be a reality. She would contract Additions Inc., a small-scale home building company, to do the job. Since her father had worked for them she knew they were a strictly no frills outfit that simply did good work.

Leanna looked up at the hunter green sunshade with white tassels above the patio and drew in a deep breath. The scent of honeysuckle filled the air. It felt good to be out here, recovering from her sprained ankle! Bryce had advised taking a week off to recoup and return when she felt better. That would be tomorrow. In today's report she'd told him that her ankle felt fine and she couldn't wait to get out of her enforced idleness.

She sorted through the rest of the mail, mostly bills. Then she stood up and pressed her foot to the floor. It felt good. Relieved, Leanna pushed the patio door open and went into the kitchen to fix roast chicken sandwiches and salad for lunch. The large kitchen clock showed one. When Alice came by to drop off Kai, they could all sit out on the patio and eat lunch.

She took out thick slices of roast chicken from a medium-sized plastic container, set them aside, and then made a salad.

A car pulled up outside. They were here, just in time for lunch. She arranged slices of wheat bread in the toaster.

Leanna heard Alice's quick tread and Kai's short, shuffling one and opened the door.

"Hi, there." She bent down to hug Kai. "Have fun at the daycare?"

Leanna smiled at Alice. "Lunch is ready. Why don't you stay and eat with us?"

"Love to."

They all piled into the kitchen. "Help me carry the plates out to the patio." Leanna handed plates and napkins to Alice.

"Mommy, can I play with Cody?"

"After lunch, sweetie."

Sandwiches made, and the salad tossed, they sat down to eat on the patio. A bullfinch fluttered busily near the bird feeder.

"My loan's come through. I can start work on the snack bar."

"What about your job with Bryce." A meaningful glint showed in Alice's eye.

Leanna didn't want to think of what she'd have to tell Bryce when it came time to take over her new snack bar. "I'll have to stay till I finish it. Once the contractors finish working on The Tug, I'll have to leave to run the snack bar. I hope my work with Bryce and the remodeling finish at the same time."

Leanna watched Kai munch on her sandwich vigorously. She knew her daughter wanted to be finished with lunch and play ball with Cody.

"If you're through eating, you can go and play. Looks like Cody is anxious to run out." She patted Cody's head and he stood up with his tongue hanging out.

Kai crumpled her napkin and laid it on her plate. "C'mon, Cody."

"Now." Alice leaned forward, a conspiratorial look stealing over her face. "What really happened on your first day at work?"

"If you want to know if Bryce proposed marriage to me, you can forget it. We had a rip-roaring fight."

Alice looked disappointed. "No! And I was hoping…"

"You're wasting your time." Leanna's mouth set in a determined line. "We don't have a meeting of minds. Or anything else in common." Her heart raced as she remembered the kiss they shared. If she reminded herself often enough that they had nothing in common, maybe she could stop her heart from doing cartwheels whenever his name was mentioned

"Oh, but you do." Alice put her work-hardened hand on Leanna's. "Your child."

"He doesn't have to know that."

"Aren't you going to tell him?" Alice's eyes opened wide in shock.

"I can't…yet."

"Then when?"

"I…I don't know."

Alice's face tightened into an expression of sympathy. "Sorry, I'm doing it again. Asking questions, when I know I shouldn't."

Leanna gave her an encouraging smile. "Thanks for caring about Kai and me."

"You're easy to love."

"Thank you, Alice. Don't worry about me. I'm a big girl now."

Leaving the island after that eventful night hadn't been easy. Wondering and guessing if the aviation fuel would arrive on time kept her temper short, and as if she didn't have enough to worry about, the thought of spending another night in proximity to Bryce had the ability to charge her senses and make her light headed.

Leanna took a sip of her lemonade. "I was glad when the fuel plane finally arrived. That was my ticket to get home."

"Was Bryce sorry to see you go?" Alice asked in a teasing voice.

"I don't think so. I was a liability." Leanna remembered the grim expression around his mouth as he helped her up the portable steps placed by the side of the plane.

She knew they'd both chosen to ignore the episode of the night before. At least, she could see it in his cool manner.

The warm sunshine poured over Leanna and Alice as they sat back in the wicker-back chairs and watched Kai and Cody chasing each other.

Leanna folded her napkin and let it drop onto her plate. "I'd better see about the loan today, and then call Additions Inc. about the remodeling."

"You're a busy gal this afternoon."

"I want to get it all done so I can head back to the island tomorrow."

"Need any help with Kai?"

"No, just with The Tug. Once the remodeling is complete, I'll take over. You've been a great help, Alice."

"Chester's been spending quite a lot of time at The Tug. So I've not had to be there too much."

"I'm glad Dad's been helping out with the store." Maybe Chester would start to notice Alice. No harm in hoping! Still she didn't expect him to come out of his reclusive state easily.

Alice got up and shook out her tunic-style blouse. "I'd better be going. Thanks for lunch." She gave Leanna a hug and went around to the front where her car stood parked.

After Alice left, Leanna went indoors and called Additions Inc. to let them know that she wanted a remodeling job done.

"My father will give you the measurements, since he's familiar with all that," she told the chief contractor and owner of the company. "And you can start the job anytime."

"Next week suit you?"

"That'll be fine." Feeling relieved, Leanna hung up the receiver. At least now the contractor was on standby to do the job. Now to call Citywide Bank about the loan.

* * * *

"I'm taking you on some field work today." Bryce's eyes crinkled as he welcomed Leanna with a broad grin.

She got off the plane with a light step. After several weeks, she was better able to cope with the flight to the island. Today, the lake appeared greener than usual, the sky bluer than her previous plane rides. Even though her fingers gripped the hand rest of her seat, she breathed easily. Curiosity about what work Bryce would have her do filled her mind more than the agitation about flying.

"Don't you want anything put into the computer today?" Leanna looked around at the familiar, floppy duffel bag lying in readiness to be picked up and hauled along.

"That can wait. I want you to see something of what we do." Bryce barely looked at her, appearing to be preoccupied with gathering the equipment and shoving folded sheets of paper into his pocket.

"Are we using the plane?"

He looked at her and grinned. "No plane this time. We're walking."

For a moment, they stared at each other as if Fred and the student assistants did not even exist. Bryce turned abruptly to pick up his duffel bag. "Better get going."

"What about Kip?" Leanna had just seen him going into the shed.

"He stays here and holds down the fort. Besides, he has his own thing to do. We pay him to keep the plane in tip top condition, which is what he'll be doing, I expect."

As the sun climbed higher in the sky, a haze sifted in through the clump of trees. In the distance, toward the Ridge, it lay like a translucent canopy.

Fred and the student assistants walked on ahead, carrying a contraption of some sort.

"What's that they're carrying?" Leanna pointed at them.

"Number four foot locks to catch wolves with. No, don't look so alarmed. They're not like bear traps where the bear has no way out, and the only outcome is pain. Once we get one, we earmark them, examine their teeth to determine age, and inject them against parvo virus. After that, we radio-collar them and let them go."

"That's good to hear."

"We set a few of these within the home range of the wolves."

"Home range?"

"Where the wolves are likely to be found according to previous studies."

Leanna walked alongside of Bryce, taking longer strides than she usually did, trying to keep up with him. A surreptitious glance at him revealed the quickened pace of his breathing, and his eyes gleamed with the hidden excitement that his work obviously gave him.

"You do like your work. I'll give you that," Leanna muttered.

He let out a loud guffaw. "That's the closest you've come to giving me a compliment, Leanna." But the surprised manner in which he said it implied he didn't laugh it off as easily as he pretended.

"I like to give credit where it is due." Leanna concentrated on the trail, which grew less clearly marked now. They entered deeper into the woods.

"Set one right here," Bryce called out to the threesome ahead of them.

"You got it," somebody replied.

"What happens now?" Leanna asked.

"We wait and then split up to see if we've caught any wolves, examine them, inoculate them, and let them go." He looked at her. "Tired?"

"Of course not."

"Okay, no need to snap my head off. You feminist women!"

"Feminist! You wouldn't even begin to understand the meaning of the word."

"Whoa. Don't get so rattled because the word defies definition. Remember, we're out in the woods tracking wolves. One thing about you, you're not predictable. Onward." He pointed ahead with his index finger and waved her on.

Leanna walked on, furious at herself for losing her calm and letting him see her vulnerability.

"You know what you remind me of?" Bryce held a map with odd markings as they resumed walking.

"No, what?"

"A female grouse. In early spring, the male does a dance to impress her. There he stands near the chopped off cherry plants nearby, purple throat sacs distended, wings outstretched, beating the ground in a frenzied dance. Out there in the clearing, the grouse lek, as it's called."

"So how does that remind you of me?"

"By just being you. You think you have this power over me, don't you?" He moved toward her and gave her a caressing look.

"Whatever you're thinking, you're wrong."

"How would you know what I'm thinking?"

"I can tell when you're trying to find a parallel between us and something totally different. I'm not a female grouse and this is not a mating dance," Leanna said with fire in her voice.

He laughed. "We are all in the same scheme of things, whether bird, animal or human. Which means, we're all doing a ritual mating dance in one form or another. For instance, take you and me, out here in the woods. If you didn't have your armor of wariness about you to protect yourself, where would you be?"

"Don't flatter yourself, Bryce." She whirled around and stared at him, her hands on her hips. "My wariness is not an armor I wield against you or anyone else. I have my priorities laid out clearly."

Bryce held up his hands. "Okay, okay. Seems to me, you protest too much." He took a step back and leaned against a tree, his arms crossed. "Just what are your priorities, Leanna? Kai, for one, I think. You're a good mother."

She threw him a quick glance, her chest thumping like a noisy fire engine at the mention of Kai. "Thanks."

"What's the matter? Are you surprised I should say that?" A look of curiosity skimmed his face.

"I'm just surprised you'd have anything complimentary to say about me, that's all." Leanna willed herself to calm down and wondered if this would be a good time to tell him about Kai. No, he was just paying her a casual compliment. What had come over her? Her vanity about being a good mother lay like a dormant volcano wanting to spew out a magma of premature revelations. She had to overcome her need to be patted on the head where Kai's well being was concerned.

"What's going on in that head of yours?"

Bryce's voice jolted her from her thoughts.

"It's for you to find out if you really wanted to," she said, trudging behind him.

"I'll find out one of these days. And then I'll have you all figured out," he said.

"Why's it so important that you should figure me out?" She couldn't resist the slight dig.

"I ask myself that, and I can't come up with an answer," he said. There was a dullness in his voice that surprised her. "And when I figure you out, then I'll also know why you ran away." He stopped and looked back at her, then walked slowly toward her, his features mirroring the convolutions of his thoughts.

"I've told you all you need to know, Bryce." She looked directly at him even though the sunlight pierced her eyes through the trees.

Bryce let out a breath and shook his head with heightened impatience. "Some landmarks here signal the dispersion of the wolves," he muttered. He glanced at his map and then looked around him, his forehead furrowing. Work claimed his attention now. He looked as if he was walking in a trance following the trail that would lead him to wolf dens.

Fred and the student assistants were several hundred yards ahead of them. In the distance, through the foliage, Leanna saw them stop and unload their bag.

"Looks like they found a site to place one of the footlocks," Bryce said, squinting through the afternoon glare. "Better keep away so they can do their job. Two set so far. One to go."

"And then what?"

"We go back to the first one to see if we've got a wolf." Bryce folded the sheet of paper and jammed it back into his pocket.

* * * *

Two hours later, sweaty from walking miles in circles, Leanna and Bryce lugged themselves back to their starting point. A wolf lay nestled among the soft leaves of a ground level shrub. "There he is," Bryce said in a whisper.

He motioned to Leanna. "You stay here, while we sedate him."

After an eternity, when she had begun to amuse herself with following a flitting yellow butterfly, Bryce called out to Leanna. "You can come now."

She walked over to where they huddled. Fred and his assistants got up as she approached them.

"All yours, Bryce. It needs your special touch. We're off to the next one."

Fred shouldered his duffel bag and disappeared into the greenery with the two men following behind him.

The wolf lay, looking almost like Cody curled up in his corner of the room. She had an urge to cuddle him. "He looks cute, asleep like that."

"He's under sedation now. I'm about to draw some blood for testing. This one is clean, no parasites. He's a yearling. His mother must have been fairly healthy; he's got her immunity."

Leanna watched him, fascinated by both the gentleness with which he administered the syringe and the look of fondness that played on his face as he examined the wolf's ears, teeth, and paws. "How calm he looks."

"That's just what I was thinking."

Bryce worked in silence for a few minutes as Leanna watched the strong tanned hands gently turn the sleeping animal. She couldn't help staring at the confident way in which he handled his work. A warm feeling enveloped her as she marveled at his expertise and gentleness.

Leanna shuffled in her crouching position uneasily. "Need any help?"

He looked up suddenly, an expression of surprise on his face. "Thank you, no. I might need you to carry something later." He looked at the wolf's coat in sections. "I'm almost done here. The sedative will be wearing off soon, so I'm going to set him free. See this collar around his neck? It's got metal studs to prevent another animal from wrenching it off. It will also send beeps to an antenna we have on the plane. This way we keep track of him."

"Radio tracking?"

Bryce nodded. "We've also ear-marked him. See?" He pointed to the inner skin on the wolf's ear. "His number is T15."

"You do know your job."

"And love it too." Bryce unhooked the foot lock and gently prodded the wolf. "Still asleep, thank goodness. We'd better go."

"It's the job, not the place that calls me," Bryce said as they walked to the next site. "Which means that when my study is done here, I move to where the study takes me."

That's more than clear to me, Leanna thought, *which is why you and I don't have too much in common.* With a baby coming, she'd wanted a family, security, and Bryce's love like a lifeline, not a nomadic lifestyle.

"And you, Leanna? It's just the opposite, isn't it?"

"That's exactly right. For me, it's the place, Pelican Harbor. It's where I belong in more ways than one."

Bryce let out a heavy sigh. "Too bad."

"Why do you say that?"

"Because maybe we could have had a chance together."

They walked along side by side. Despite being tall herself she came up only to his shoulder. She stared straight ahead, not wanting to look at him. If she did, she might fail in her resolve not to be led by sentimentality.

A cuckoo chirruped as they edged along the narrow trail, Leanna walking dangerously close to him. A ledge-like promontory stood mocking as Bryce led the way and Leanna followed. One slip of the foot and they'd cascade like dribbling rocks to the sandbar below.

"Better hold on to my hand." Bryce held out a hand behind him.

She could take her pick between the danger of his physical closeness or the plunge of fifty feet below. She extended her hand, fingers outstretched and he enclosed it in a strong, firm grasp.

"Come on. Follow me." His footsteps left a mark on the soft earth.

"Do I have a choice?"

"Drop the editorial for now. We have to get up the hill first before we can come down to the other side."

Something pricked her pride. "I'm slowing you down, is that it?"

"You're tired," he said with a sigh.

Twenty minutes of muscle-tightening climb later, they reached the flattened top of the hill. Down below, on the other side, was a trail they had to follow. Their steps quickening, they walked on, while Bryce whipped out his map again.

"Straight ahead."

But when they got there, Fred and his assistants were waiting, looking as if they'd lost their best friend.

"What's up?" Bryce said.

"We set this up a long time ago. But we haven't got a wolf."

Bryce shrugged. "We'll take what we have. I don't want to leave the foot lock here unless we're in the vicinity to monitor it."

"You mean we walked all the way up the hill for nothing?" Leanna asked sharply. The next moment a feeling of shame washed over her. She probably sounded like a petulant child.

"We wouldn't have found out that we didn't get a wolf if we didn't get here, now would we?"

In the next site, to their relief, a wolf waited to be sedated and examined. Leanna watched Bryce, savoring each moment. He is easy on the eye, she thought. The incline of his head, the steady fingers working deftly as he radio collared the wolf, his hair falling on his forehead riveted her attention.

She wakened from her daydream when he spoke. "All right. All done. Off you go, boy." He unlatched the foot lock, opened up the muzzle and then stood up. "When he awakes, we'll be out of here."

Leanna hadn't realized the afternoon sun had weakened as they hiked back to the cabin in the same configuration they had set out. Fred and the two men were walking quite a way ahead of them.

"It's way past lunch time," Bryce said. "Hungry?"

"A little. But I can eat when I get home."

"Are you in a hurry to get home?"

"If you don't need me for any more work." This would be a good time to tell him about her loan and the work on the snack bar. "I've taken out a loan to build an addition to The Tug. I'm having a snack bar added on."

"I'm impressed. Quite the businesswoman, aren't you?"

"Which means as soon as it is complete, I'll have to leave work here to manage it." She looked straight at Bryce to sense his reaction.

"Now, who's the workaholic? Just be sure you finish the work I give you now." His gaze held her for a second. "As soon as our work is completed, we'll be leaving."

"Where will you go?"

"Minnesota, Washington State, wherever there are wolves to be monitored. You, however, are anchored here, I take it."

"This is where I belong. You and I are in different orbits now. You shouldn't have come looking for me, Bryce." She said the words that were inevitable.

"Yes, I know." He walked on without turning to look at her, his profile a strongly etched study.

It caused her a twinge of pain that he had accepted her remark so easily. Part of her knew there was no chance that they could have a life together and part of her wished desperately that they had.

When she finally saw the dark brown log cabin she felt as if she were meeting a much-needed friend. Ever since she started working here, she felt a camaraderie with its unconventional environment. But one person took away her composure. Bryce. Still, why worry about that? She'd be leaving to manage The Tug and the snack bar soon enough. But then, another little worry cropped up in her mind. That this might be the beginning of the end.

Chapter 9

Leanna watched from across the faux marble counter top as small knots of customers straggled in, filling the tables laid out in twos along the length of The Tug. Additions Inc. had done a marvelous job of constructing the snack bar.

It was a curved addition to the original gift-store structure. An entire wall had been removed to allow more space for a deli section with seating and a counter from where food could be served. A side door led outside, where a few more tables were arranged under a brightly colored awning. Most customers gravitated to this outside seating area with its hanging flower baskets and clear view of the lake.

"Hi, there." Leanna smiled at a young couple that wandered in holding hands. They, no doubt, didn't care where they sat, just as long as they could gaze into each other's eyes. They walked to one of the window tables, still hand in hand, seated themselves and ordered a chicken salad sandwich and coffee.

Leanna smiled to herself. Ah, the foolishness of young love! It petered away like a distant echo. How well she knew young love, another name for infatuation.

She glanced at them from under her lashes and put together their sandwiches. How old could they be? He might be twenty-one and the girl looked nineteen. Leanna remembered her first love, a one and only love, some sweet memories, others bittersweet, but all valuable to her as life experiences. Best of all, she had Kai, for whom she was grateful.

"Need any help, dear?"

Leanna looked up from the cutting board holding sliced onions and celery for sandwiches. Alice stood in front of her in a print dress and a saucy straw hat.

"No. Thanks for asking. How's it been at your end?" Leanna had only a vague impression of people going into the gift section.

"I had people looking at the copper artifacts."

Leanna's gaze caught the copper model of the Luddington mine hoist, which sat on a wooden ledge near the window in the gifts sections. Prominently displayed, it had elicited questions from tourists. Pelican Harbor used to be a boomtown during copper mining days, she'd tell them, hence the miniature mine hoist.

"And how are *you* managing the fetching and carrying?"

Leanna's face contorted into a grimace. "I'm sure my feet will have to pay the price. But I wanted this."

"You sure did. And worked hard for it. You'll do fine." Alice's voice sounded soothing and mellow like the soft afghans she was always crocheting. "I'm surprised Bryce didn't mind."

"My work there is finished."

The young couple, who had asked for chicken salad sandwich, seemed to have forgotten their order. But Leanna hadn't. Too well she knew that people couldn't live on love alone!

"Here's your order. I'll bring your coffee."

She poured out coffee in two mugs and brought it to them.

A few more customers wandered in and stared at the view from the window before seating themselves.

"How soon summer's gone." Leanna's gaze flitted toward the open window behind the coffee pot.

The tall maples fronting the houses in the distance were starting to turn color. When had summer drifted into early fall? She hardly remembered the number of times she'd been flown over to the island to work on the wolf-monitoring data. The trips had become a matter of routine, and the flights there hadn't bothered her at all anymore. Most of the time she'd concentrated on chewing gum while looking out the window at the curvy contours of the lake and land below them, thinking about the charts she'd have to draw up that day.

"Have you heard from Bryce?"

Leanna's chest hammered. "No, and I don't expect to. He's busy trying to finish his work." Her mind suddenly threw into focus the image of Bryce and Fred collecting boxes containing logbooks, syringes, ropes and other odds and ends. The scene was etched in her mind.

"When do you leave?" Leanna had asked him, managing to inject a casual pitch to her voice. Watching them packing to leave created a strange feeling in her mind, like seeing migratory birds disappear forever, despite Nature's promise that they would return when leaves appeared on the trees again.

"As soon as we radio collar a few more wolves. We've not done too badly. For a while there we thought we might not get the ones we'd targeted." Bryce's strong, golden-brown hands pulled on the ropes as he coiled them neatly and set them in piles. Watching him brought back memories of being in his arms, feeling secure and loved. Even a glance at him engrossed in the most ordinary chores sent her senses reeling.

The clatter of cups and saucers brought her back to the present and she realized Alice was talking. "I don't get it. You're head over heels in love with the guy, and you won't do anything about it. Are you going to let him go again?"

"Alice, I'm not in love with him."

"And I'm a tea kettle." Alice's whisper came out in a hiss. "You've been going around with a stricken look the past week. If you didn't have The Tug you'd go stark, raving mad."

Leanna couldn't help chuckling at the ferocity of Alice's remark. But surely, Alice was wrong! Leanna felt no throbbing, languishing pain in her heart, and as far as she knew, she ate like a horse and fell asleep as soon as her head touched the pillow. Ergo, not in love. Of course not. Was she?

She shook her head with exaggerated vigor. "No, no, you're mistaken. Besides," she said quietly, "Bryce doesn't love me."

"Aha, now we're getting somewhere." Alice sounded triumphant.

"He doesn't belong here. And this is where I want to be. This is where I grew up. This is my home."

"You could work something out."

"There's nothing to work out. So let's just forget it." Leanna's voice rang with finality, which, she hoped, would clue Alice that the subject was closed.

* * * *

Leanna puttered back and forth from the wood shed to the back porch, hauling in wood for the fireplace. She'd stack the logs near the door within easy reach, where she could lay her hands on them when the weather became chilly.

The big maple out back threw an ever-changing shade on the cement floor of the porch where Chester had piled wood in a neat heap.

Leanna tried not to think of her aching feet. Customers had streamed in steadily at The Tug, both in the store section and at the snack bar. She smiled as she thought of Alice throwing her a wide-eyed look with her hands held open. Leanna knew what she might have said if she were standing closer to her: "You wanted this!"

If the volume kept up, she'd have to hire a teenager to man the store section and have Alice help her in the snack bar. Leanna had finally convinced Alice to accept wages for working at The Tug. So it was all fair and square, giving Leanna a feeling of satisfaction.

She held the back door open with her foot as she carried the logs inside, balancing them precariously in her arms.

"Get out of the way, Cody."

Cody had been following her in and out the door like a forlorn puppy. "You're bored because Kai's gone over to Cecily's, aren't you? And you're never going to forgive her for leaving you home."

Cody cocked his head to one side as he sat watching her. Then he got off his haunches and edged closer.

"No, Cody! Watch out!"

Two of the logs, thick heavy ones, tumbled out of her arms and fell on Cody, who let out a yelp of pain. He crouched and dropped to the floor, his cries becoming louder and more pitiful.

"Oh, baby," she cried, dumping the logs on the floor and crawling over to where he lay whimpering. "Your poor tail. Don't move, sweetie. I'll find a bandage." Blood dripped onto the carpet.

She pushed herself up. If only she could keep calm. Cody was just another baby—her second child, and her heart ached whenever he got hurt.

The First Aid box was in the bathroom cabinet and she hurried there. She pulled open the lower cabinet door under the sink and snatched the green box that held anything she might need for emergencies. Leanna sucked in her breath, hoping she'd find a bandage thick enough to contain the bleeding. She rummaged furiously through the box and found a roll of bandage. Not enough by a long shot, but it would have to do until she thought of what to do next.

She glanced at her watch. Six thirty. Would the vet's clinic be open? They usually had an emergency number to call. Maybe somebody would answer if she called.

She ran back to Cody, knelt down and started bandaging his tail. "Yes, I know, sweetie. We'll make you all well."

A dull fear settled in her chest and she stared at the blood spurting out. What if the bleeding didn't stop?

Leanna placed as many gauze patches as she'd managed to grab and bandaged his tail. She had almost finished when the roar of a vehicle reached her ears. Sure that she had secured the bandage, she got up and moved to the window.

A lean tall man swung out of a jeep. She drew a breath and watched him stride to the door. Bryce! What would he be doing here on the mainland at this time?

She flung open the door and pulled him in. "Oh, Bryce! Cody's hurt!"

His gaze strayed to the far end of the L-shaped living room and Cody lying near the wall.

"Cody, what's the matter, boy?"

Embarrassment mixed with misery swept over her as she watched him walk toward Cody, her face tear streaked and her hair askew. Her clumsy hold on the logs had inflicted this awful condition on poor Cody.

"I was carrying logs and t-two of them fell on Cody's tail."

Bryce walked in the door and closed it behind him.

"Cody," he said in a low voice as he moved toward him and knelt down. Cody licked his hand with a piteous look on his face and Leanna watched, feeling limp and helpless.

"I did the best I could with the bandages." She squatted on the floor beside Cody and patted his head while he looked up at her with a look of utter devotion, even through the pain.

"We should get him to the vet. Is he open at this time?"

"There's an emergency number to call." Leanna hurried to the phone and dialed the number. A cool female voice, utterly devoid of emotion, answered. But when Leanna told her the problem, a modicum of feeling and concern filtered through the phone line, and she told her to bring Cody right away.

"The vet is there. We can take him now." Leanna looked over her shoulder at Bryce.

"Let's get him to my jeep." Bryce bent over him. "Come on, boy."

Leanna ran into the kitchen and groped in the treat jar for Cody's favorite doggy treat in the shape of a bone. She brought it to the living room and held it in front of him.

"Come on, sweetie, we're going for a ride."

Cody raised himself with great effort and followed alongside of her. "That's a good boy."

Bryce held the door open for them. "I'll bring the jeep." He hopped into the jeep and drove it as close to the front steps as he could manage.

He got out and lifted Cody in, making sure his tail was out of the way of his grasp.

"There. Now he can lie down on the seat."

"He loves car rides." Leanna, seated in the front, turned back to look at Cody, who had settled into the seat, obviously not interested in looking out the window today.

Leanna sat staring out the window, grateful for the breeze on her face while they drove in the mellow embers of the evening. Her mind settled with a feeling of relief. Bryce was here. He was a thorough professional with wolves, and now he was gentle with Cody, just as she'd expected. He took charge of things without the slightest hesitation. How close she felt to him! When this was over she'd tell him so. Tell him? More like throw her arms around him and plant a kiss of thanks on that inviting mouth.

"Tell me where to go," Bryce said as he steered the jeep down the road that led from the hill onto the main highway.

"We'll have to pass the business district," Leanna said, glancing back anxiously at Cody, who now lay with his face on his paws in the back seat.

Bryce kept his eyes peeled on the curving road as they approached the business district then left it behind them.

"The sooner he gets taken care of, the better." He turned and threw Leanna a look of concern. "And how are you doing?"

"Okay, I guess. To think I always worried he'd get a glass sliver in his paw running at the beach."

"Where's Kai?"

"At Cecily's. Just as well. She'd cry her eyes out if she saw poor Cody in this condition."

They arrived at a low roofed brick building with a wooden statue of a dog by its entrance. A sign that said "Cole's Vet Clinic" slid into view.

Bryce parked the jeep, jumped out and opened the back door. "Come on, baby." Leanna coaxed Cody with a bit of dog biscuit.

He got up, tottering a little.

Bryce held out his hand to him. "Come on, Cody. There's a good boy."

Cody got off the seat in one slow-motion jump and Bryce wrapped his arms around the length of him. "Hold still for me, Cody. I'm going to carry you in."

Dr. Cole waited near the reception counter.

"I got here as soon as one of the veterinary technicians gave me the message. Bring him in here." He opened one of the examination rooms.

The vet put on his gloves and undid the bandage, now completely soaked. Holding it gently, he examined Cody's tail. "There's a deep cut that will require stitches under sedation. It's better if he stays here overnight instead of going home with you," he said. "Would you folks prefer to wait outside while I treat him?"

Leanna nodded.

"Do you want me to stay with Cody?" Bryce whispered to her.

Her eyes brightened and she nodded. A wave of relief and warmth surged through her. Who better than Bryce to stay with Cody? She remembered the expert way in which he'd examined and vaccinated the wolves. He could easily double as a vet. Leanna put her hands on him and he encircled her with his arms.

"Would you? That would be helpful." Leanna felt her body go slack with gratitude.

Helpful for whom? Not for Cody. He'd be under sedation. And Dr. Cole would probably have an assistant in with him to help him. But it relieved her mind to know that Bryce would be there as well. She needed that assurance.

"I'll see you later," he was saying, but she barely heard him.

Leanna moved to a chair in the waiting area and, as she sank gratefully into it, she scanned the notices on the bulletin board. A German shepherd with puppies waited to be bought, a collie needed a new home because his owner was moving away. And Cody was in the examination room getting stitches on his tail because she hadn't watched her step. How fortuitous that Bryce had showed up. His gentleness and concern were a salve to her now, just when she could use it.

Leanna let her head rest against the high back of the chair as she waited. Maybe she could tell him about Kai today. He'd changed a great deal more than she'd realized, not just in his appearance, but also in the surprising sensitivity he showed when dealing with sick animals, and herself.

But was she ready to share Kai with him yet? Something held her back. Mother love, possessiveness, whatever. The days and nights she'd watched Kai play, sleep, talk to her dolls, and wondered if she'd ever know her father were too numerous to count. The chance to bring them together stared her in the face now. Leanna's eyes closed, heavy with tiredness and from crying. Silence reigned in the small clinic, except for the muffled sounds of Dr. Cole talking to his assistant. Leanna heard a series of short yelps from Cody, and then, silence. A shot of sedative had obviously quieted him.

Leanna's head lolled to one side on the back of the chair and she shut her eyes as images of Bryce's quick action and loving care for Cody swept through her mind. Leanna's pulse quickened. Maybe she could trust him with her heart, and maybe it was time to tell him about Kai. Guilt from keeping this secret was eating her up inside and she couldn't let that go on. She rubbed her aching temples trying to come to a decision. It would be the right thing to do, she thought finally. Telling Bryce about Kai.

Chapter 10

"Leanna, wake up." Bryce's deep, velvety voice penetrated the waves of sleep that had overcome her, and she shook herself awake.

"What?"

Dr. Cole stood behind Bryce, smiling at her. "Cody's doing fine. It was a deep cut, and from the bandage, I see that he lost a lot of blood. I had to put in nine stitches. He'll be a little groggy tomorrow, but otherwise all right after a night's sleep." He looked at Leanna, kindness radiating from his eyes under ragged white eyebrows. "You can stop worrying and get some rest."

"Thanks for your help. I'll pick him up tomorrow."

Leanna followed Bryce out the door to the jeep. Darkness had fallen and lights winked on either side of the road as Bryce put the jeep into gear and backed out of the parking lot. The inky blue air felt crisp and dry.

"After I drop you off, I have to meet Kip at the Park Service office," Bryce said.

Somewhere in the back of Leanna's mind, a question popped up. "Lucky for me you happened to come by."

"Actually, I couldn't find a file. I came to ask you about it."

"I combined a couple of files so you'd have the text and the diagrams all in one packet."

He nodded, his eyes scanning the road. "It's okay. I'll check on that later."

"Do you want me to come over and find it?" Leanna didn't want him to think she was sloppy in her work.

"No, I'll look for it. Besides, I'll have to unhook and dismantle the computer soon. There's no point in your coming to the island, just as long as I know where to look for the file."

He turned to look at her. Aided by the white streetlights whizzing by, she could see the finely drawn set of his face.

"How's your father? I haven't seen him since he took us to the island when we first got here."

The question jolted her, coming suddenly as it did. "He's doing very well, as long as he has carpentry projects to work on. He loves keeping busy."

"He dotes on you. I could tell even talking to him that first time."

Leanna smiled. "We're a lot closer since Mom died."

"You're lucky." He let a sigh escape his lips. "I think I told you I never knew my dad." When Leanna nodded he said, "He left us, my mother, kid brother and me, one fine day. He just walked out of our lives. And I thought that sort of thing happened only in the soap operas. I was only eleven, but even then, I decided to take over as head of the family. Mom had to take what work she could get to keep us fed and clothed." His voice trailed away, his left hand resting on the steering wheel, and his right on the gearshift.

A sudden charge of sympathy billowed out of her. Obviously, he'd been carrying the memory of his early years for a long time.

"You told me some of it, but not how you felt." A note of regret colored her voice. Why didn't he confide in her those times they'd been together?

Now they sat side by side, a pair of strangers trying to know one another all over again, as if those in between years hadn't happened.

"Seeing Mom slave like that was too much for me. I vowed then that I'd work as hard as I could, and take care of her and my kid brother, too."

Leanna heard the undercurrent of hurt in his voice, and her own reaction of admiration surprised her. She watched him, wonderstruck. "But why didn't you say something? Anything."

"I suppose bitterness and resentment held me back. I still had to get over that." He forced the words out in a low whisper.

The road slowly traversed uphill and it curved toward the lane that led to Leanna's house. Lights glistened like gems in between the foliage far to the left, the side of the hill that rolled away to the lake, now calm under the clear night sky.

Leanna felt a strange tug at her heart and she stared unseeing at the dark road in front of them. She'd never seen Bryce like this before, never knew what he'd carried around with him in his innermost mind. If only she'd known, she'd have understood him a little better, been less self-centered.

"It meant a lot to me to finally give Mom the nice things she'd been doing without when Ray and I were growing up. And she never complained."

He slowed the jeep and turned a sharp corner. Ahead, Leanna saw her house, where she'd set the living room lights to go on at dusk.

"What was your mom like?"

"Hard working, ambitious for us kids."

"Like you."

"She was both mom and dad to us. God knows we needed it. Surprising how she kept her sense of humor during the hard times."

He slowed down the jeep, swung into the short driveway, and parked it at an angle.

"Thank you for helping with Cody." Embarrassment filled her when she thought of her reaction to Cody's affectionate behavior with Bryce and the childish scene she'd made. Her voice grated with tiredness and she pulled herself out of the jeep.

"You sound dead tired. Need any help?" Bryce said.

"No, I'm fine...er, would you like something to drink?" Cola, lemonade, an apology? She scolded herself mentally for lacking the foresight to restrain herself from past outbursts with him.

Bryce pressed his watch to check the time and Leanna saw the pinhead glow of its face. "I have about half an hour before I meet Kip at the Park Service office."

He picked up his cell phone tucked in the holder between the two front seats. He put it into his shirt pocket, got out of the jeep, and followed her up the steps.

Leanna dug her hand into her jeans pocket and, fishing out her keys, opened the front door. The living room was lit.

"The lights are set to come on after dark," she explained, smiling at Bryce's surprise.

"Good idea."

"Please make yourself comfortable. What would you like to drink?"

"A pop, if you have any."

Leanna left the living room, catching a glimpse of Bryce looking around the room with growing interest. She opened the refrigerator door and peered inside. Covered Tupperware bowls and assortments of breads and flavored yogurt cartons met her eye. But no cans of cola lay in the jumble of bowls, cartons and plastic bags. She'd forgotten to buy some after she and Kai had finished the last one yesterday, and she hadn't had time to run to the supermarket.

She glanced at the one-gallon carton of milk. He could have milk. That would constitute a nice, cold drink. She poured out a tall glass of milk and returned to the living room.

"I'm, sorry, but there's only milk," she said handing the glass to him.

He took it and threw back his head and guffawed.

"What's so funny?"

"I'm right about you. You never fail to surprise me."

Leanna smiled. "A good surprise, I hope. I remembered you like milk."

"Thanks to Mom, who dinned it into my head that milk is the most nourishing drink." He finished it in one swig and placed the glass on the coffee table.

"You must have been thirsty."

He walked to the tall window overlooking the lake. "I've never seen the lake from a distance like this."

Leanna walked up beside him and followed his gaze toward the lake. "Yes, it's free and it's beautiful."

He turned toward her and moved closer, so that she could feel his sweet breath on her. "Like you. Maybe, that's why you still intrigue me so much."

He held her gently by the shoulders and drew her closer and lowered his mouth onto hers and took her breath away in one long, demanding kiss. Surprise quickly changed as Bryce held her close. All her previous longing flooded her as she slowly entwined her arms about his strong shoulders and returned his kiss with fervor. As much as she fought herself, Leanna knew this was what she had wanted ever since Bryce swept back into her life. It was crazy, but somehow she couldn't make herself react sensibly. She wanted Bryce with her whole being.

He led her to the couch in the living room. It stood there, inviting, coaxing. She froze.

"Don't fight it, Leanna." Bryce's voice assumed a new tenderness as he pulled her down.

Fighting this feeling was the farthest thing from her mind. Leanna knew her emotions were out of control. For so long she'd fought against loving Bryce. Would it hurt anyone but maybe herself if she gave in tonight?

She laid her head back on the soft cushions and ran her fingers through his hair, felt his mouth seeking hers. She'd forgotten the number of times she'd wanted to feel the thickness of his hair between her fingers. The spicy soap he'd obviously used filled her with unabashed desire. For once in her life, Leanna decided she would be selfish and take the love Bryce was offering, even if it were only for this small moment in time.

"You're really something, Bryce Robertson." Leanna felt her heart beat to a new refrain. Slowly, she unbuttoned her blouse and felt his hands move along her skin. She loved him and she was darned if she was going to restrain herself any longer. His hands found her jeans buttons first, and then, his belt buckle.

Her hand reached out to dim the lamp near the head of the sofa. His hard body was atop hers and she welcomed him. They made love as they had never before, listening to each other's rhythmic breathing intermingled with the sounds of birds settling for the night outside. His ardor was touchingly restrained and she gasped in sweet agony as she writhed beneath him, eager to touch his skin.

Out of nowhere, it seemed, a phone rang. Leanna knew it wasn't hers.

"My cell phone." Bryce got up and moved to the armchair where he'd thrown his shirt. Fumbling in the pocket, he drew out his cell phone.

Awkwardly, Leanna pushed herself up from the couch. The euphoria of moments before slowly faded into cold reality. Bryce's abrupt switch from lover to scientist brought a chill to her skin. It just proved to her that as strong as her love for him was, he hadn't changed. He still put his work first. Now what she had to decide was whether she could live with that. Regretfully, she didn't think she could.

"Yes." He ran his fingers through his hair. "I'll be there in a few minutes," he said snapping the phone shut. "That was Kip. He's ready to go."

Bryce walked back to her, pulling her to him, caressing her hair and body. "God, I don't want to leave you. For the first time, I don't want to go back to work. That's the effect you have on me."

Leanna winced. As much as she wanted to believe him, the proof was in the fact that he was leaving.

"That's an achievement for me—distracting a workaholic like you. Something I never expected to hear." She knew she shouldn't consider it a triumph, but she couldn't help it. Their lovemaking had been sweet and she reveled in the thought of it and didn't want to let him go. But, this time, a toughness steeled her. As sweet as it had been, she wasn't about to hold him with any strings just because she had been hypnotized by his touch and the memory of his fiery kisses.

She watched him run down the steps and into his jeep and wondered why she hadn't told him about Kai. She had intended to, but she'd let herself flow along with the sweet tide of their passion. She'd wanted to hold that moment in her hands. As she thought back she remembered there hadn't been any words. There was no time for words when love flowed in her like warm honey, when they had both yielded to the searing need, which had been building for months.

Leanna got dressed and straightened the couch and the cushions, a smile careening across her face. Now the couch had history. Its archaic green and brown upholstery looked deceptively staid, not the venue of unbounded passion. So much for the lessons of restraint she'd always imposed on herself. But did she have any regrets? No! She only savored the feelings of satisfaction he'd left behind.

* * * *

The rain beat down in long mercury-colored bullets, washing away the dust left by the summer months. Hitting the roof of The Tug, it kept up a steady background rat-a-tat to the sound of voices in the snack bar, creating a cozy atmosphere inside.

Tourists had started leaving Pelican Harbor in dribs and drabs. But that hadn't stopped the stream of customers in Leanna's snack bar. These were Pelican Harbor's own folks, who had now found one more place to spend a pleasant hour or two chatting with friends. She hoped when the ski hill opened in the winter, her snack bar would overflow with enthusiasts stopping for hot chocolate and buttered croissants.

She glanced at Chester happily fielding the gift store section of The Tug, chatting with customers, regaling them with salty sea tales, playing the Ancient Mariner to the hilt.

"Dad is in true form today, Alice. Do you have something to do with that?" Leanna grinned.

She went around the small table behind the snack bar to pour coffee refills for everybody. But not before giving Alice a sly look. Her father had been close mouthed about it all, but Leanna knew when something perked up his life. He sang more and became less broody. Further, his well-worn cap did not sit atop his head at a rakish angle anymore. Instead, he combed his thinning white hair and slicked it down with pomade.

"Okay, Alice, what's going on?"

"What do you care? Seems like you've been wrapped up in another world even though Bryce is clear across the lake." Alice threw her an elf-like grin. "And if you want to know, all I did was make your father a lemon meringue pie."

"Yes, I heard about how good it was. And then I asked him what he was going to do about it." Leanna chuckled when she thought of the number of times she'd dropped atom bomb-sized hints to Chester about taking Alice out.

"Why should I do that when the woman doesn't care a rat's tail about me," he'd said when he'd stopped at her house to put up the storm windows.

"You'd be surprised. Dad, you should know she has a crush on you."

"Sometimes, women have crushes for the wrong reasons."

"And how many have you gone out with? Go on Dad, give it a try. Ask Alice out. You can't be a recluse for the rest of your life."

"And what about you? Seems to me that young Robertson guy has been on your mind lately."

"Now, how would you know that?"

"I'm your dad. It's my job to know things. By the way, when are Bryce and his crew done with their work?"

"Any day now." And that had dragged her spirits down and she'd clutched her cocoa mug tightly to will away that plummeting feeling. That had been a week ago.

"He took me out to the Gandy Dancer. Said how good my meringue pie was." Alice's hands flew with effortless ease while chopping up lettuce and tomatoes for a club sandwich for the last customer. "Did you know your father's a good dancer?"

"Yes, when he's in a mood for it." Leanna laughed. So her father *was* kicking up his heels, thanks to Alice. "You're good for him."

The miniature wooden steering wheel-shaped clock over the entrance showed five o' clock. Pulling out her jacket from the small, cubbyhole backroom of the snack bar, she said, "I have to pick up Kai from Cecily's. She had lunch there after daycare. Could you and Dad lock up?"

Leanna reveled in her idea of throwing Alice and Chester together in seemingly inadvertent ways. Top-level diplomacy could take a tip or two from her!

Alice nodded. "See you later." She picked up a cleanser and a rag from the cabinet to wipe off empty tables before starting to lock up.

"See you later, Dad." Leanna smiled and waved to Chester.

He looked up and grinned. "You take care of yourself."

Leanna walked out to her car, pleased as a cat dozing in a cat condominium. Things were moving along nicely between Alice and Chester. And the sparkle in his squinty eyes told her that his life had started to pick up for him.

Leanna revved up her car and sped out of the parking lot, beating the evening traffic. When she reached the main road intersection, she turned right to go the short distance on the lilac tree-covered drive to Cecily's.

The little girls engrossed in playing in the sand box looked up at the sound of Leanna's car. Cecily stared at her friend's mother, her little mouth drooping at the corners.

"Kai will come over again. Or maybe you can come to our house," Leanna said and walked Kai to the car.

"Cody's waiting for us at home. I didn't take him to The Tug so he could rest his tail."

Leanna found her way back to the intersection. Good thing they were only a hop, skip and jump away from the Lake District. The frenzy of the rush hour traffic even in a small town like Pelican Harbor had grown conspicuously. And that was a good sign.

Turning off the road that ran parallel to the lake, she slowed down and entered their driveway.

"There's Cody!"

Sure enough, he stood on the armchair, like a picture framed by the window.

Leanna parked her car, helped Kai haul out her Gummi Bears school bag and together they walked up the steps. She opened the door and found Cody, a broad smile on his face, prancing about.

"Is Cody all better now, Mommy?"

Leanna glanced at his tail. The bandage had been removed and the fur that had been shaved on the injured part was now coming back.

"Yes, he is, thank goodness."

They both sat down on the carpet and Cody rolled on it like a spirited adolescent dog regressing into puppy hood.

Seconds later, the phone rang and brought their romp with Cody to a crashing halt.

Kai sat up. "Shall I get it, Mommy?"

"No." Leanna got up on her knees. "I'd better get it."

She moved to the phone on the side table, grabbed it and sank back onto the floor. "Hello? Bryce? This is a surprise."

She hadn't heard from him since that evening on the couch. She darted an involuntary glance toward the piece of furniture that sometimes served as a makeshift trampoline for

Kai and Cody. "If walls could speak" took on a new meaning for her.

His voice sounded light. She could almost see him smiling, the fine laugh lines crinkling the corners of his eyes. Now, thinking of it, those eyes had a perpetually amused look. "I called to tell you I found the file I was looking for."

"I'm glad." Relief swept through her. Despite her show of confidence, a part of her had hoped that she hadn't lost it to the Cyber Bandit.

"Are you all packed and ready to go?" Leanna held her breath, waiting for his answer. Did she really believe he would stay? No, of course not, but that didn't stop her heart from aching with pain.

"Almost. We're running out of food. Makes no sense to stock up again, just for one or two days."

An idea struck her like a boxer's punching bag. "Why don't you guys come and have dinner with us the day you move your things to the mainland? I could whip up something."

She wanted one last chance to see Bryce; she couldn't get used to the idea of his leaving for good. She brushed the back of her hand against her forehead while she concentrated on her thoughts. No, she thought, that wasn't it at all. She just wanted to be hospitable and offer him and his crew a good meal.

"We do have to shack up at the motel our last night at Pelican Harbor. We'll have the jeep and a rented car to haul our equipment back to Wisconsin…" He paused. "If it isn't too much trouble…"

Trouble? No, no trouble, she thought, but maybe she needed her head examined. To put herself through the heartache of watching Bryce leave was a crazy thing to do, even though she looked forward to seeing him again. It was like being pulled in two completely different directions.

Now heavy disappointment dragged her down. He talked as if he had already forgotten their sweet moment of love making, when, for her, it was everything, unsure though she was at the time at the rightness of it.

She bit the inside of her cheek and said nothing.

"Leanna, are you still there?" Bryce said. "I've been thinking of you."

"That's very flattering, but given your situation at the island, I hardly think it's me."

"Still cynical. No, I have to say it's you, ma'am. Moreover, you're a liar." A soft chuckle accompanied his words.

Leanna's heartbeat jumped. "Now that's a strong word."

"That evening, at your house, your actions belied all the words of protest you've uttered." A laugh tinkled at the other end of the line, reminding her that she'd been nothing but a little hypocrite. The way she'd responded that evening in his arms had surprised even her.

"Okay, you win. I can't deny it meant something to me." Did it mean anything to Bryce? His tone was light, almost joking. Her cheeks flushed with shame. She'd practically thrown herself into his arms. She didn't regret it, not for one moment, but what about Bryce? What was he *really* feeling? Perhaps, seeing him one more time would tell her if they had a chance together. And after that, she didn't know what would happen. She'd wait to find that out when she told him about Kai.

"Look, I know my work takes me to strange places, but you have to realize we had something that evening," Bryce said.

"It was just one evening."

"It told me what I wanted to know. Anyway, we can talk about it when I come see you for dinner the day after tomorrow."

Leanna let out a breath of relief. Bryce felt something for her. The few times they'd been together had shown her that. Maybe they could work things out. Furthermore, family was important to Bryce, something she hadn't realized nearly seven years ago.

"That's when you're moving to the mainland?" Leanna asked.

"Yes. It will take several trips transporting us and our equipment across."

"We look forward to seeing you."

"That, I believe, is the formal way of putting it. Will you?" Again, the teasing inflection in his voice.

Leanna gave a low laugh. "You'll just have to wait and see for yourself."

"Always the lady of mystery." He accompanied his remark with a wolf whistle and then hung up.

Leanna put the phone back in a pensive mood. She had finally reached Bryce as never before. She saw the things that were important to him and they were the same ones that she held dear. Surely, he'd understand her reasons for not telling him about his daughter sooner. She'd had to walk a long road in her own comfort level in being able to broach the topic to him, and now that her destination was in sight, she applauded her own decision of telling him about Kai.

Chapter 11

Bryce pitched a ball of twine into the cardboard box ready to be hauled onto the plane. Then he went into the kitchen area and threw open the cabinet doors above the sink for one last look. Bare shelves met his glance. Good. The student assistants had emptied the shelves and carted the stuff away with them on Kip's first foray back to the mainland.

He turned around and saw Fred fold a tarp and pack it in one of the other cardboard boxes.

"All set?" Bryce lifted the box to estimate its weight. "Good thing we don't have many more of these to take. Did you make the arrangements at the Overland Motel?"

"Uh-huh. Told them we'd be overnighting it and then heading out from there."

Bryce had toyed with the idea of shipping the equipment while they drove the jeep back. It would be a tight squeeze with all of them packed in like dill pickles. But then he decided against it; he wanted to keep the equipment where he could see it, and have it reach Racine the same time they did. If he had to, he'd rent one more car. The generosity of the research grant would allow him that.

Bryce could hear banging and thumping outside. That would be Kip closing up the storage shed. All specimens had been transported to the Wildlife Center in Wisconsin in ice-lined containers, and the shed cleaned out and disinfected.

Bryce strode out the door. "Ready when you are, Kip."

"I'm ready." Kip grinned, looking like a gnome with his woolen cap pulled tightly over his head. "Let's see if I have it right. I'm to drop you fellas on the mainland and then I'm free?"

"That's right. Don't forget the dinner tonight at Leanna's place."

"That'll be a change. Some nice home cooking." Kip's grin grew even broader.

"I guess we're all ready to head back to civilization." Bryce thought of their cramped quarters where moods could veer toward crankiness. All in the interest of science, a fine cause. "Move it, Fred." He looked into a room where his colleague still appeared to be fidgeting with a long sheet of cellophane.

Fred lifted the box and followed them into the plane. "Good weather," he said looking up at the sky.

The men loaded the remaining few boxes onto the plane and got in. They strapped themselves in while Kip revved up the engine and started the propeller.

"And we're off." Kip taxied a short distance before lifting off.

Bryce watched the trees soon dwindle to the size of bushes. He'd never get used to this even though Kip's expertise as a pilot was beyond belief. Bryce sat back in his seat and decided to enjoy the shiny mid-morning view over the lake. He shut his eyes and tried not to think. But Leanna sneaked into his thoughts. He remembered holding her in his arms, hot with passion. An ardor he hadn't expected burst into flame quickly, and he pulled on his plaid shirt collar. They'd been good together. Passion and youth, a steamy combination. Bryce swallowed, his throat thick and dry. They weren't kids any longer, but passion was as strong as ever, together with a new respect for the roles that each played in their respective lives. Thinking of her, he felt as if a blast of steam had hit his face. He'd forgotten what it was like all those years ago, but the nuances of their time together painted an ever-brightening picture in his hope-filled mind. Surely, they had a future together now.

His gaze scattered over the scene outside, but it could be a bowl of soup for all it registered in his mind. He still smelled her perfume and wished he knew the name of it. Bottom line was that he couldn't forget her.

He forced himself back to the present and glanced at the top of Fred's head in the seat in front. He suppressed a chuckle. Just as well Fred couldn't see his goofy, moonstruck expression, which was probably what he had at this very moment.

The drone of the plane lulled him and he laid his head back on the headrest, closing his eyes. An image of Leanna filled his mind and a feeling of heady anticipation rose inside, dispelling his earlier lethargy. Now he was confident he'd be able to sort out the confused feelings that had filled him these past few days. So, okay, she didn't talk about Kai. Probably thought it was none of his business since he wouldn't know the father. He was crazy to think she'd even let him be a surrogate father to the little girl. It didn't really matter to him who Kai's father was, she was Leanna's daughter and that was all he cared about. More than once, he'd wondered how things would stand if Kai were his child. It was a nice fantasy, but he knew Leanna would never have left him if Kai were his child. Well, he'd soon see her and this time he wouldn't leave until they settled things between Leanna and himself.

Twenty minutes later, the plane touched down at the familiar landing site near the Park Service office. Bryce waited for it to stop taxiing, then undid his seat belt. He kept his head bent as he got out of the plane.

"Hand me the stuff. I'll stack it in the office until we rent the car," Bryce told Fred while Kip logged the mileage in a logbook.

"We'll drop you at the motel and then we're off to get the rented car," Bryce said.

"Suits me."

They were all a little cramped in the jeep. But Kip had only a short ride to the Overland Motel.

"Hang on." Bryce turned the key in the ignition and backed out of the parking lot with more zip than necessary.

"Taking revenge on me, huh?" Kip asked, visibly startled at the sudden jolt.

Bryce grinned. "We'll miss you, guy."

As they drove toward downtown he saw the Overland Motel, unpretentious and sparse. It would do just fine for the night, being only a few minutes' drive to Leanna's house from there.

He let Kip off at the front entrance. "Be ready for dinner tonight. I'll give you a ride over to Leanna's."

Bryce revved up the vehicle again and drove to the car rental office a few blocks down.

* * * *

"Hand me the butter," Leanna told her little helper who was standing on a step stool by the kitchen counter. With a dab of flour on her nose and streaks of it on her curls, Kai looked comical.

Leanna knew how important Kai felt helping her prepare dinner for Bryce and the crew this evening.

"Here, Mommy." Kai handed her the bar of butter solemnly. "What's that for?"

"For the sauce to go with the asparagus. Then, there's ham, baby carrots, and Boston brown potatoes." Leanna recited the menu more for her own satisfaction than for Kai's information.

Leanna wiped floury hands on a blue apron and glanced at the ham through the lighted window of the oven. Nice and golden brown, and the potatoes she'd roasted over the stove gave off a delicious buttery aroma. She sprinkled a pinch of dill over them and stood back, admiring the whole effect.

Leanna reached up and pulled out the plates from the top shelf of the cabinet. There would be eight adults, including Chester and Alice. Cody would sit near them and watch, but good manners would prevent him from begging for food.

She ran a damp cloth across the dining room table and spread a fresh off-white tablecloth on it, before arranging plates with napkins and silverware. The guys would probably appreciate a sit down meal, instead of one perched on some handy piece of furniture, with plates balanced on their palms.

Leanna glanced at the clock. An hour and they would be here. She'd told Bryce to come at six o'clock. If she remembered right, he'd insist that his associates be punctual. Alice and Chester were arriving a little early.

"Time to get ready," she told Kai. "Here, let me wipe the flour off your nose." Kai looked comfortable enough in her corduroys and turtleneck, but Leanna needed to get out of her sweats. A long wool skirt and a slim sweater would be just right for the evening.

* * * *

"For you." Bryce thrust a slim bouquet of pink carnations into Leanna's hands and looked around the living room. "Come on in, men. Don't be bashful."

His Harbor Girl

He turned to Leanna, his glance lingering on her longer than was necessary. "We've lived in the backwoods for so long we don't know how to behave in polite company."

Leanna laughed and stood aside to let them in. "I know you're all hungry, so what d'you say I serve dinner?"

A chorus of assent went up. "Yes, anytime."

"Need any help?" Bryce followed Leanna into the kitchen and leaned against the counter.

His lean, tall figure standing in her small kitchen momentarily mesmerized her and she remembered the first time she'd seen him standing in The Tug. How long ago had that been?

"Must you stand there like that?" The words came out before she could stop them.

His mouth quirked in a grin. "Why, Leanna, I believe I'm unsettling you. Never thought I'd have that privilege."

"What I meant was, if you really want to help, you can carry the dishes from the oven to the dining room," she said and deftly moved out of the way, letting Bryce carry a water jug ceremoniously to the table.

The truth was the alarming closeness of him bothered her. It hit her like pin pricks and sent a thrill down her spine. At the same time, the weighty problem of how she'd actually tell him about Kai laid her spirits low. Would he think she was a conniving person for keeping Kai's true identity a secret from him this long? But then, their relationship didn't seem to be going anywhere. Leanna wasn't sure that the beautiful, full blaze of passion that had happened between them was enough to make their love last a lifetime.

She heard Bryce's voice and shook herself free of her thoughts. "I'm just getting warmed up, milady. You don't know the maitre 'd I'm really capable of being."

"I can guess," Leanna said over her shoulder, wondering if somebody would like barbecue sauce with their meal. This was as motley a crew of people as she'd ever had at her place, and she'd seen the lumberjack appetite these men were capable of. "You can put the salad on the table. It's in the refrigerator."

"Yes ma'am." Bryce trotted back and forth between the kitchen and dining room, the epitome of meekness.

At Leanna's next pass through the kitchen, he caught her by the waist. "Not so fast. I have a proposition to make."

"Now? This minute?" Leanna took a deep breath and moved back against the counter to face him. "This might not be the best time. I have a dinner to serve."

"I agree. Just preparing you. I'd like to see you privately later tonight. We've got to talk."

She needed to talk to him too. About Kai. "I think I can arrange that. Alice and Chester are staying to help clean up and then they're taking Kai out for an ice cream." Leanna smiled, thinking of how Kai took matters into her own hands and asked Chester to take her out for ice cream to Baskin Robbins.

"May I say you look lovely?" His gaze glided over her.

"Thank you."

Leanna went into the living room. Chester, relating his yarns, had the men in gales of laughter. She never knew how much of it was true and what he'd made up. But they did the trick of entertaining listeners. "Time to eat," she said.

In a flurry of activity, people found their seats. Crisp white napkins were unfolded and the dishes passed around.

Assaulted by hunger, Bryce's associates concentrated on their food.

Bryce attempted conversation on their behalf. "You'll have to excuse them. Their silence is really a compliment to your cooking."

She grinned. "I'm pleased."

"Anytime," Kip said.

She caught sight of Alice gawking at Bryce. No doubt, she was still reeling from the presence of the tall, handsome Bryce in Leanna's home, a place that functioned as a second home to Alice.

"Are you gentlemen coming back here anytime soon?" Alice asked.

"It all depends on where my next study takes me. I have a couple of options." He looked straight at Leanna.

I'll bet you have, Leanna thought. Her mind was fast-forwarding to how she'd broach the subject of Kai to him.

She twirled her fork around the stem of her asparagus. Looking up, she caught Bryce giving her a pointed look that jogged her back to the present.

"Bryce, will you take me in your plane sometime?" Kai's voice prodded Leanna's thoughts.

"I promise, someday I will. I haven't forgotten." A smile brightened his face.

He obviously really liked Kai. The way his attention engaged when he talked to her gave him away.

"Anybody for dessert?"

"Thought you'd never ask." Fred grinned.

Alice got up to do the honors. The dessert was her department. She'd brought in a spectacular Bundt cake, which caused her audience to salivate.

"That's the best cake I've ever seen." Chester followed her to hand out the quarter plates for dessert.

Leanna grinned to herself and watched her father turn domestic and content, something her mother could never get him to do. Years ago, he'd been bitten by the sailing bug. Now it looked like another sort of bug had bitten him, the devoted family man.

Fortified with the plates of Bundt cake, everyone sidled over to the living room to find comfortable spots to enjoy their dessert. Bryce sat on the carpet with Kai to continue their discussion of paper airplanes, Cody forming a furry backrest for Kai.

"Keep an eye on the time, fellas." Bryce looked up from his paper airplane project briefly. "We need to load the vehicles."

"We're leaving right after dessert." Kip briskly polished off his plate with his fork.

"Right," Bryce replied. "You can take the vehicle we came in. I'll get a ride back to the motel." He looked at Chester. "Could you drive me over?"

"Anytime." Chester started picking up the plates. "You want that ice cream now, Kai?" He darted a glance at Kai.

"Yes, Grampa."

"We'll have to wait until Alice and your mother finish up with the dishes."

Alice snagged Leanna in the kitchen while they soaked the dishes in warm sudsy water.

"How can you let that gem of perfection out of your sight?" Alice adjusted her glasses and stared at Leanna. "You shouldn't let him go."

"You mean Bryce?"

"Who else? You know you're batty about him."

"I don't know about letting him go, but I do know I'm going to tell him about Kai. Wonder how he's going to take it." She bit on her lower lip, wishing she hadn't waited this long. Her feelings had been so muddled that she'd wanted them to settle before she told Bryce anything. Was there ever a right time to tell a man that the child he's known for a few months really belonged to him?

Leanna wiped the dishes as Alice handed them to her squeaky clean and hot from soaking in the water and then rinsing. She stacked them neatly in the kitchen cabinet, wiped her hands and then glanced at Alice.

"All finished. I don't know what I'd have done without your help tonight." Leanna smiled at her friend. "And the cake was delicious. In fact, it's all gone."

"That's the way I like it." Alice found a towel and wiped her hands briskly. "And now, we're off with Kai."

"Sweet of you and Dad to take Kai for ice cream."

"It's not just Kai. Your father likes it too. Who's he kidding?"

Leanna laughed and gave her a hug. "Enjoy the ice cream, you two."

Fred, Kip and the student assistants were ready to leave.

"Thanks for a great dinner and a pleasant evening. Your daughter is a charmer." Fred acted as spokesman for the four of them. "Just like her mother."

"Thank you, Fred." Leanna liked this gruff, uncomplicated man.

The two students didn't say much, but gaped at her.

"Hope you liked the food," she said to them. Their painful shyness puzzled her. No doubt, working in the labs and in the woods only heightened it.

"Oh yes," they said in chorus.

"See you fellas later." Bryce saw them to the door.

Minutes later, Chester and Alice fetched their jackets. Leanna helped Kai on with hers.

"Have a good time, honey." Leanna buttoned her down filled jacket.

"Bryce, are you leaving Pelican Harbor?"

"Yes, tomorrow." He bent down and straightened her collar.

"Aren't you coming back here no more?"

Bryce glanced at Leanna and straightened up. "I don't know, Princess. But if I do, I'll call and tell you first. How's that?"

"Okay," Kai replied in her piping voice, seeming perfectly happy with that arrangement.

"Good." Bryce guided her gently toward the door where Alice and Chester stood waiting.

"I'll drop you off at the motel when we get back," Chester said.

"Thanks." Bryce followed Leanna to the door, his hand at her elbow.

Alone together, after what seemed like an eternity, they fell into each other's arms.

"I thought I'd never get you to myself," Bryce murmured as he drew her close, smoothing the hair away from her face. "I've missed you."

"Me too." Leanna wound her arms around his strong neck and leaned closer, sniffing the scent of his aftershave. Dizzy with the heady feel of his body, she closed her eyes and buried her face in his neck. "We have to talk."

"In a moment. First things first." Bryce drew her head back gently and closed his mouth over hers. She felt his warmth and tenderness easing into her senses.

A second later, she drew herself away from him.

"I need to tell you about Kai," she began, holding him with a steady gaze. "She's ours. Yours and mine." Leanna saw no other way of saying it, except with unerring directness.

His eyes widened and he stared at her, a look of utter disbelief flooding his sharp features.

"What did you say?" His body taut, the tender expression of only moments ago had died. In its place, bewilderment turned his face into a stony mask.

"I'm sorry I couldn't tell you sooner. I did try to. I honestly did," Leanna said, moving away. How futile it sounded even to her. Except, she knew she had tried at selected moments to tell him, but it had never been the right time.

"You couldn't tell me sooner?" His mouth thinned with displeasure. "How could you keep something like this from me?" He paced the room, obviously trying to absorb what she'd just told him.

"I'm sorry it had to be today, just when you're leaving." Leanna's hands clenched and unclenched.

"That's just it. When I'm about to leave town. Were you hoping I wouldn't have time to think of what to do next if you caught me in a hurry?" A muscle flicked angrily at his jaw and Leanna flinched at the tone of his voice.

"It wasn't like that." Leanna crossed her arms across her chest, feeling her spirits come crashing down.

"Then what was it? I've been here for months; you've worked by my side, yet you couldn't tell me Kai was my daughter? I find that difficult to accept."

She had expected his anger, but even so, that didn't make it easy to face it. He wasn't going to forgive her. So where did that leave them? And what about Kai? If their relationship had a chance before, it didn't have one now. It frittered into embers before it had a chance to blossom.

He shook his head as if he didn't want to listen to her anymore, causing an aching misery in her heart. "I'm through trying to understand you. How could you do this, Leanna? You not only deprived me of my daughter, but her of a father. Does she know? No, of course not. You didn't want to share our daughter. Did you think I wouldn't sense it? Every time I tried to get close to her, you stiffened, telling me with your body language to back off. I deplore the fact that Kai has to go through this." Bitterness rang in his words and his face flushed with anger.

Something snapped in Leanna. Obviously, he had decided that she'd schemed all along for some obscure reason. "Whatever the outcome of our relationship, I'd never have deprived Kai of a father. I had to work out when to tell you." She managed to keep her voice calm, but she could feel it rising several decibels in an effort to vindicate herself.

"When it came time for me to leave?" Spoken quietly though they were, his words rang out like gunfire ricocheting around the room.

"I wasn't ready before this," Leanna said, knowing she had the courage of her convictions on her side.

He strode to the chair on which his jacket lay and picked it up. "Kai means a lot to me from the little I've come to know her. But, you, I've got to get some distance from you."

"Fine!" Leanna felt the blood rush from her face. "I'm to blame for everything, as usual," she said and took a step back as if stung by his words.

"Perhaps, you were getting back at me for thinking you had a child by another man, when ostensibly you and I were together." His features assumed an expression of mask-like impenetrability and he looked away from her.

"Your suspicions were hurtful, Bryce," Leanna said in a hushed voice, remembering her disbelief at the time. "And I couldn't face them."

"My suspicions! What did you expect, given the circumstances."

He turned to face her with a weary look and Leanna felt herself go slack, suddenly indifferent. Maybe it was a defense mechanism she'd cultivated.

"Think what you like," she said. "I need my space too."

A sharp ring jabbed through the room.

Bryce felt his jacket pocket and pulled out a cell phone. "Hello? Fred?"

"Didn't know if you still needed a ride. I could come and get you if you do. We're done loading the vehicle."

"Yes. I think I'll need a ride back to the motel." Bryce clapped the phone shut and jammed it back into his pocket. "I want my child, Leanna. Make no mistake about that, but I'm too angry right now to discuss this. You'll hear from my lawyer in a few days."

"Your lawyer," she asked, fear making her voice wispy.

"You'll need child support. And I want access."

Leanna took a step back, stung by his words. "I couldn't take any money from you, Bryce, but thanks for the offer on Kai's behalf. You don't need a lawyer for access."

Her worst fear was coming true. She was losing her child and had already lost Bryce. He thought her the worst schemer he'd ever laid eyes on. She had no chance for any semblance of happiness, having lost everything she considered valuable in her life.

"So now you're going to veto my offer. Are you being quite fair to Kai?"

Leanna clenched her hands together. His offer hit her like a sudden thunderbolt. However well intended, she couldn't accept it the way things stood between them.

"That was not my reason for telling you about Kai." She too needed distance from him to think things over, as obviously he did.

He stood by the window and looked out. "Fred should be here soon. That'll save Chester the trouble of dropping me off at the motel. I'd better get back to make sure the equipment has been loaded properly." The words came out in a matter of fact way, as if the argument over Kai had never taken place.

Leanna turned away, overcome by confusion. But Bryce seemed to show no indecision. He would leave and that would be that.

"I guess…this is goodbye," she said, her throat constricting. A dullness invaded her, and it grew, despite her will to ignore it.

"I'm afraid so. When I came here, I had hoped I could make some reparations for what happened years ago. But I see that the blame is not all mine," he said.

Leanna looked at him, her misgivings increasing by the minute, for what she saw in his eyes looked like cold distrust.

"Then nothing I can say or do will make you think any better of me." She drew back into the room as he reached for the doorknob at the distant sound of a car approaching the driveway.

"You'll hear from my lawyer. Don't fight me on this." His gaze held hers for the last time, and then he turned away and disappeared into the night to the waiting car.

Leanna closed the door, the ache in her heart chilling her to the core. Why did his reaction hurt her so? Because even the worst she'd expected wasn't this—that he'd hire a lawyer. Now all she could do was wait with foreboding and hold on to Kai for as long as she possibly could. Would she lose Kai's affection as well? Fear and misery sank her into a stupor. She hadn't planned it like this.

She heard a car drive up. Chester, Alice and Kai were back from having ice cream. And they would find Bryce gone.

The door opened and Kai tumbled in, followed by Chester and Alice.

"Hi, Mommy." Kai looked around. "Where's Bryce? I want to show him my pretend volcano." She brandished a small purple volcano, the type that came with boxes of cereal. Leanna had once filled one of these with vinegar and baking soda and watched the wonder in Kai's face as the "lava" bubbled over.

"He had to leave, honey. He asked me to say 'bye'." Leanna helped Kai remove her jacket and hung it up in the closet.

"Why'd he leave? I was going to drop him off at the motel." Chester's scraggly eyebrows rose. No doubt he was trying to make sense of Bryce's unscheduled departure. Leanna understood Chester's respect and liking for him.

A dry laugh rose in her throat. Everybody liked Bryce. Too bad she and he couldn't get their lives to mesh together.

"Fred came by and picked him up. Bryce wanted to make sure the equipment was loaded in right," she replied with a benign smile. No need to let on what had happened, especially when Alice picked up things like radar.

"Too bad. We could have chatted some more." Chester shook his head.

"You like him, Dad?"

"You bet. Can't understand why…" He stopped and glanced at Kai who wilted like a drooping flower. "Time for bed eh, little girl?"

"Good night, Grampa." Kai hugged him and Alice and scuttled off to her room.

Leanna hugged her father and Alice, and saw them to the door. "Goodnight. And thanks for the help."

She tried to ignore the query in Alice's eyes as she walked down the steps holding onto Chester's arm. Leanna managed to keep her composure. She'd think about the hollow feeling in her throat later, after Kai dropped off to sleep.

Leanna went into the kitchen and poured herself a cup of still-hot coffee. The first sip somehow revived her. Tomorrow she'd pick up the pieces and get on with her life with Kai.

Chapter 12

"It's yours if you want it." Jim Koeppel, the director of the Wildlife Ecology Center in Wisconsin, pushed a letter across the desk toward Bryce. "The Board is pleased with your work and would like to offer you the directorship when I retire."

Bryce grinned. "That's very flattering. But I'm no administrator and my work is out in the field."

"Your work on the wolves is getting a lot of attention, Bryce. Make the most of it."

"Meaning?"

"Someone like you at the helm of the Wildlife Center would create all the publicity it needs for Federal funding. Because, let's face it, the bottom line is the important thing when it comes to the viability of an organization." Jim's face lit up with a smile obviously meant to coax Bryce.

Bryce laughed. He liked the kindly, dignified man, who would soon retire as director, and who had just paid him the compliment of naming him as successor.

"Thanks for your trust in me, Jim. But I have to decline the offer. Besides, I'm moving to the State of Washington to do a gray wolf study there." As far away from Leanna as possible, at least for the time being, until he sorted out his mixed feelings.

"None of my business, Bryce, but is something the matter?" A look of concern crossed Jim's age-lined face.

Bryce looked up from the paperweight he'd been handling idly. "Why do you ask?"

"Seems to me, you've been preoccupied since your return from Pelican Harbor."

A grim smile quirked his mouth. "It's a personal matter which I've been trying to sort out."

"A matter of the heart?"

Bryce nodded, reluctance making him cautious.

"I see. I can understand that. I've had first hand experience, when I nearly lost Madge to another man."

He got up as Bryce rose to leave. "I hope you'll reconsider the offer of the directorship." Jim gave him a pat on the shoulder.

"I certainly will. But I don't know that I'll think any differently about it. Thanks all the same." He moved toward the door.

Bryce left the whitewashed building, Jim's words about the directorship ringing in his ears. The ache and longing was far worse than anything he had experienced before. The bright intellectual chasing after his life's ambition was now stagnant with heartbreak. Such a thing was possible, as he was finding out. No one could hurt him like Leanna; he knew that now. And Kai. God, how he missed her! He wondered if Leanna had told Kai who he really was. He wondered, too, if Kai was hurt he'd left so abruptly.

Bryce inserted the key into the ignition with a sharp motion and turned it, and then turned into the busy main thoroughfare. He tried to concentrate on the traffic lights. But images flashed in his head just as surely as if they were beating against the windshield of his vehicle. Images of Leanna sitting at his computer lost in the meaningless data he'd thrown at her. It was a wonder she didn't have to get reading glasses, considering the hours she spent inputting tables and figures. And the way Kai loved being carried so that she could pretend to be taller than he.

Bryce drove as if the jeep was on autopilot, except his knuckles stretched tight over the steering. What was he thinking when he'd mouthed words that could have only caused her pain?

* * * *

Leanna watched as the mug filled with frothy hot chocolate before she shut the tap. She noticed with satisfaction that the cold weather brought more and more customers into the snack bar. She had Carly, the new girl, helping her. Alice's talent in running the gift store had resulted in increased sales.

Leanna handed the mugs of hot chocolate to a couple of young men from the lumber company across the road. She then wiped down the counter top and put away the rag.

Yes, things were definitely picking up at The Tug. By dint of hard work, she'd made herself a successful businesswoman surrounded by her family. So what if an unfulfilled aspect of her life lay before her like a long stretch of empty road? She'd get over not seeing Bryce again, given time.

Customers started to leave. She'd extended the closing time to six o'clock and it pleased her to find them lingering until the last moment.

"I'm bushed," she said to Alice. She wasn't sure how much it had to do with being busy and how much with missing Bryce. The hollowness in her heart just didn't seem to go away.

"Why don't you go home? I'll lock up."

"Thank you, Alice. Ready to go, Kai?"

Every afternoon, after daycare, Leanna would pick up Kai, and together they'd go home to have lunch. And then they'd bring Cody back with them to The Tug.

"I have good news." Alice's eyes grew round with delight. "Chester and I are getting married."

Leanna whirled around from the window she'd just secured.

"That's great," she said, giving Alice a hug.

"Thank you, dear. It took some doing." Alice beamed, happiness flooding her face.

"I can imagine! Dad isn't one to take a hint. When's the big day?"

"Not sure." Alice put the tray back and locked the cash register. "You're the first person I've told."

"Alice is going to be your new Grammy," Leanna said, helping Kai pick up her toys.

"Will you come visit Mommy and me after you be my Grammy?"

"Of course. Always and forever," Alice assured her. She glanced at Leanna. "What about you?"

Leanna let Kai and Cody walk on ahead of them and stood by the door. "There's nothing about me. I told Bryce about Kai."

"How did he take it?"

"He was pleased that Kai is his daughter. But me, that's another matter." Leanna grimaced, thinking about the hard set of Bryce's jaw when they'd talked last.

Alice shook her head. "Maybe it'll all work out. Fingers crossed."

Leanna said nothing and walked out the door to catch up with Kai and Cody. It would take more than crossed fingers for her life to straighten out, for the heartache to heal. Only, this time, there was much more to heal.

His Harbor Girl

* * * *

Leanna picked up clothes, cutout dolls and colored markers all jumbled together in Kai's room, and sorted them, placing the clothes in a neat pile. A picture on the floor caught her eye. It showed Kai's unmistakable choice of bright colors. Another one of her "family" pictures. It had a man, a woman, a little girl, her hand on the head of a large dog. The man and woman were holding hands, and behind them shone an enormous sun, its rays almost touching the people in the picture.

Hand pressed to her face, she stared at it. Now Kai was consoling herself with drawing pictures of the family they could have been. A heaviness loomed in her chest and Leanna closed her eyes, feeling utterly miserable. She couldn't forget the happy times they'd had together—she, Bryce, Kai and Cody.

She paged through the coloring books and found more of Kai's "wish" pictures. So this was how she'd spent her time closeted in her room!

Leanna's gaze drifted to a photo of herself, Kai and Cody that Chester had taken, and then she turned away. Somewhere in Wisconsin, Bryce was continuing his study of wolves. A picture formed in her mind—the way he'd gently patted a wolf's head after the tranquilizer took effect. She hadn't missed the furrow of concern that etched his forehead at the time. He looked as if he were caring for a child being given medical treatment, and she remembered how she'd fought back the tears watching. He was no workaholic—she knew that now. He liked what he did just as much as she loved her creation, The Tug. He wanted to make a difference in the world the only way he knew how.

Despite being engrossed in chores, Leanna heard a car drive up. In the darkening scene outside, someone got out.

From the unhurried, confident walk it could only be one person. Bryce.

Her mouth opened in astonishment and she stared at him. She'd forced herself to stop thinking about him and what might have been if things had turned out differently between them. What would he be doing here now?

Leanna moved away from the window; she'd soon know what had brought him here. Maybe he'd come to take Kai from her.

The doorbell rang and she answered it.

"Bryce," she said, trying to remain calm. "Fancy seeing you again."

"May I come in?" he said, raising his voice to combat the sound of the wind ripping outside.

"Yes, of course," she answered, stepping back.

He looked thinner than the last time she saw him. Bryce had a drawn look to his face. She vividly remembered his reaction to learning Kai was his daughter, and she wasn't sure she could take his anger once again. His leaving had devastated her, and if it weren't for Alice and her Dad, she'd never have been able to pick herself up from the blow he'd dealt her.

"Did you want something, Bryce?" She felt dull and apathetic, hardly able to talk.

"I wanted you to know something and I'd better tell you right out. I'm sorry for everything I said. My only excuse is that the surprise at learning Kai was my daughter was too much to take."

The wind howled outside and created a symphony of sounds. A whirling noise rang out from somewhere in the back. It might have been from the back porch, where she stored the barbecue grill.

"I'd better go and check on that." Leanna ran to where the sound led, aware that Bryce was close behind her.

Sure enough, the tarp had flown off the grill and the lawn mower that she'd kept covered. She'd meant to ask her father to build a cover for the exposed part of the porch, but he'd been busy with his own projects.

As she fought with the tarp whipping in the wind, Leanna noticed Bryce had followed her outside. As much as she'd denied it, Leanna realized now how much she'd missed Bryce. She'd tried to get on with her life, and she had in a fashion, but something was sorely missing. She found it harder to let him go this time.

Bryce captured the runaway tarp, bringing it back, then secured it firmly over the grill and lawn mower with a rope Leanna dredged up from some corner.

"There," he said. "That should hold it." He moved toward her. "You need a man around here, Leanna."

What was he trying to tell her? She found herself hoping again, even though she knew she shouldn't—not yet anyway. Afraid to breathe in case she broke the spell, she waited for Bryce to continue.

"I came to ask you something. I've been given funding to go to Seattle but," he took her in his arms, "I told them I'd like to set up a small scale research center here in Pelican Harbor instead. After all, I have to consider my wife's lifestyle, too."

Leanna felt the uncertainty rise again every time a new hope arose. Her lips parted but she was unable to speak. Bryce solved the problem by dropping a kiss on her parted lips and holding her close, and that reassured her a little.

Moments later, she found her voice. "You...what?" Leanna looked into his eyes through a watery veil. "I didn't hear that last part."

"Will you marry me?" he said, his face softening into a smile. "You and Kai, the whole kit and caboodle."

"I never dreamed I'd hear you say that," Leanna said quietly. "But even if I agreed I couldn't let you languish here on Pelican Harbor, when you had your heart set on Seattle." Despite her caution, her spirits sang. Kai would have her father back. Strangely, in the past months, her independence as a businesswoman had seemed to matter less to her, even though she'd tried to convince herself that wasn't true.

"I can't let you abandon The Tug, after the way you've worked to build it up."

She walked back into the living room with Bryce's arm around her shoulder, feeling its protective comfort.

"I know it means a lot to you. I wouldn't ask you to give it up." The velvet harmony of his voice poured over her.

Leanna looked up, basking in the warmth and sincerity of his words and savoring them. "You…mean that?"

Bryce looked down at her, his eyes bright with love. "Of course. You put your heart into it, like everything you do." He lifted her face gently with his finger. "So what do you say?"

"Yes," Leanna said with a quiet conviction. "With all my heart."

He covered her mouth with a long kiss, and she returned it with the pent up longing of the last few months. Who was she kidding? She needed him, and so did Kai.

Moments later, she gently wriggled out of his embrace. "I have to pick up Kai from daycare."

"Allow me to do the honors and escort you. After all, we're a family now," he said.

Her heart sang to hear Bryce say those words. "Let's go together and tell Kai about us, and that you're her daddy."

She shrugged into a jacket and together, they walked hand in hand to Bryce's car.

"This is the car I drove in from Wisconsin to see you." He opened the car door for her. "And this is the car that's going to bring all my worldly belongings here to live and work with the two people I love the most."

Leanna leaned toward him and he embraced her in a quick hug.

After getting Kai, they drove home and Leanna told her about her father. The child looked at Bryce shyly for a long time as if trying to make up her mind about him.

"Friends?" Bryce asked, and he lifted her out of the car and carried her into the house as easily as one would pick up a doll. Soon, he, Kai and Cody were rolling on the carpet and Leanna stood back enjoying the scene.

* * * *

A month later, they were neither in Wisconsin nor Pelican Harbor, but in Hawaii, catching the balmy trade winds and listening to the energizing drumbeat of the dancers under a full moon.

"This is the way to escape Midwest winters." Bryce traced his finger around Leanna's ear, just barely visible in the silvery moonlight.

After the bustle of the luau festivities died down, they lay in the white powdery sand, listening to the waves lashing on the beach in front of the hotel.

"And a great way to spend a honeymoon. Make that the only way" Leanna snuggled into Bryce's shoulder, smiling to herself in the flower-scented night.

"Do you think Kai's missing us?"

"Not a chance. If I know Dad and Alice, they'll be spoiling her rotten." Leanna laughed. "But I know she'll be happy to have us back."

Bryce raised himself and smoothed back a wisp of hair on her forehead. Bending over, he said, "I'm the luckiest person in the world."

"You and me, both," Leanna said with a contented smile.

ABOUT THE AUTHOR

Rekha Ambardar has published over fifty mystery, mainstream and literary short stories in print magazines, including *Eureka Literary Magazine, Futures, The Writer's Journal, The Writing Class,* and electronic magazines such as *Twilight Times, Nefarious, Zuzu's Petals Quarterly, Writers Hood, Electronic Writers' Journal*, and a story in RFI West's charitable anthology, *Tales of the Spirit of Hope, Love, and Redemption*. She has also published poems in poetry anthologies in addition to articles in *ByLine, Bridges, Simple Joy, The Writer's Life, The National Association of Women Writers' Guide Weekly, St. Louis Writers' Guide Weekly, The Indian Express*, and book reviews in the *Ann Arbor News*.

For your reading pleasure, we welcome you to visit our web bookstore

WHISKEY CREEK PRESS

www.whiskeycreekpress.com